The Spanish Riding School Incident

Stitched in Secrets

K. L. Bordeaux

Ezra DiMarco

Copyright © 2024 by K. L. Bordeaux and Ezra DiMarco

All rights reserved.

No part of this book may be reproduced in any form or by any electronic or mechanical means, including information storage and retrieval systems, without written permission from the author, except for the use of brief quotations in a book review.

We can be found on all the usual social media sites.

Thank you for reading this series, Stitched in Secrets.

Please read our other series The Bloodhaven Manor Series which is about creatures of the night.

Chapter One

As Eliza Bennett stepped off the train at the sleek Wien Hauptbahnhof, in Vienna, the crisp autumn air whisked around her. The city pulsed with a symphony of sounds—far-off strains of operatic melodies from a nearby concert hall, the clattering hooves of carriage horses echoing lightly.

She put down her expensive cat carrier made of leather and chrome. Inside resided a grumpy orange and white tabby.

"Would you let me out, Eliza? You need to brush me, like right now," came a voice from the carrier.

"Welcome to Vienna, Merlin. You have to wait."

Merlin's tail flicked with uncharacteristic nervous energy as they maneuvered through the throngs of people. His emerald eyes danced with a light that Eliza knew too well; he sensed something beneath the typically bustling surface.

"Just think of the mushrooms, Merlin! All the shades of dye we can discover will make this trip worth it," Eliza countered enthusiastically. "My research could illuminate the threads of history that bind generations through their garments. We're in the heart of it all!"

"Ah, yes," he commented sarcastically, stepping daintily around a particularly suspicious puddle on the sidewalk. "Soon we'll be digging through the depths of botany and design."

Eliza chuckled lightly, her attention drawn to the nearby Spanish Riding School, where she knew magnificent Lipizzaner horses danced and twirled in synchronization, showcasing the beauty of dressage. Their fluid movements sparked envy and joy inside her—she longed to be part of that world. Every chance she got she took riding lessons and if the teacher offered dressage as a speciality, even better.

She'd already checked before they traveled from New York to secure a lesson with an instructor who had a penchant for moonlighting to teach outside students the art of riding.

His name was Lukas Berger and she planned to meet with him soon. Lukas had even proposed that she be an exhibition rider at the upcoming extravaganza to be sponsored by

The Spanish Riding School Incident

the wealthy Muller family. This would show how safe the Spanish Riding School methods were if an amateur like Eliza could navigate in the hallowed arena.

As Eliza settled into her quaint yet charming pension on the second floor, she marveled at the lofty ceilings that stretched into infinity. The ornate crown molding created curved patterns that whispered of craftsmanship from a bygone era. Sunlight filtered through tall windows, illuminating the wooden floors and casting playful shadows across the room. She could almost hear the echoes of laughter from former inhabitants reverberating through the walls, and for a moment, she wished her and Merlin's lives were equally entwined with the city's rich tapestry.

"Can we get on with it, dear? I require sustenance, and my dinner is long overdue," Merlin grumbled from his perch atop her suitcase. His round face imperiously demanded attention. He even lifted a paw, warning her of his impatience. Eliza sighed, knowing he was right; a cat of his stature needed proper nourishment.

"Alright, keen observer," she replied, ruffling his fur affectionately. "Let's not keep you waiting." With a quick glance out the window, her eyes fell upon a delightful little pastry shop directly across the street, its sign reading "Zuckerguss Traum." The name, meaning "Sugar Glaze Dream," was fitting, as delicate pastries adorned the glass window, enticing her senses.

. . .

"What's that?" Merlin asked, peering out next to her with his front feet resting on the sill.

"Eliza's new adventure, that's what!" she retorted playfully, already dreaming of the strawberry tarts and chocolate éclairs. "We'll get your sardines somehow, too."

A few minutes later, Eliza stepped into Zuckerguss Traum, the warm scent of baked goods wrapping around her like a comforting embrace. An elderly woman with a welcoming smile stood behind the glass display, arranging a fresh batch of cream puffs.

"Ah, willkommen! What can I do for you, my dear?" Frau Schmidt's twinkling eyes crinkled at the corners as she beamed at Eliza.

"I'd like some sardines for my cat which I know you don't necessarily carry," Eliza replied, feeling a bit embarrassed about the request. "And perhaps a few pastries for myself?"

"Never too early for a sweet treat!" Frau Schmidt laughed, as if it were the most natural thing in the world. "I have just the thing. You must try our trifles and this week's special, the Linzer Torte."

While Eliza selected her pastries, she noticed how warm and genuine Frau Schmidt felt. It was as if the essence of the bakery infused the baker with a sense of belonging.

The Spanish Riding School Incident

After collecting a small tin of sardines—much to Merlin's delight—and a box overflowing with treats, they stepped back onto the vibrant streets.

With a contented sigh, Eliza glanced over at her companion. "We've made our first friend in Vienna, haven't we?"

"Please," Merlin rolled his eyes, consuming an air of royalty, "I merely hope this friendship pays dividends in the form of high-quality cuisine."

As they strolled back to their apartment, the anticipation of exploring more of the city intoxicated Eliza. Once inside, Eliza set the pastry box on the kitchen counter, unable to resist the temptation to peek inside. The assortment of baked treasures was far too delightful. She carefully opened the lid, revealing a treasure trove of treats. "Ooh, look at these, Merlin! Just look!"

Merlin's nose twitched at the scent wafting up, his previous demands forgotten for the moment. "Very well, but I require those sardines sooner rather than later. Please, madam."

"Yes, yes, dinner next!" she promised, chuckling to herself. She looked around, taking in the space again. The walls were painted a soft buttercream, accentuating the grandeur of the tall windows that framed captivating views of the city.

"I suppose an essence of comfort is long overdue," Merlin acknowledged, finally hopping off the suitcase, his feet padding silently against the floor.

Eliza delivered the sardines to a rather impatient Merlin, who promptly settled into his new feeding station—a delicate porcelain bowl resting on a mat that had come with the apartment. As she unwrapped a Linzer Torte for herself, the soft layers filled with raspberry jam and a hint of lemon tickled her senses.

"See? Delicious treats await patient companions," she teased, taking a forkful of the rich pastry. Her tastebuds exploded with flavor, each bite a testament to Frau Schmidt's skill.

Merlin feasted with relish, but his eyes were keenly focused on the box of pastries. "You can't expect to eat all that yourself, can you?"

"Oh? Aren't we getting cheeky now?" Eliza grinned, playfully wiggling the fork in front of him. "This is just the beginning!"

"First, we conquer the culinary delights of the city, then the art," she declared resolutely.

The Spanish Riding School Incident

Merlin, now finished with his meal, washed his paws meticulously, a sign he was satisfied. "A splendid plan, my dear. Though I do hope these outings serve a purpose beyond mere indulgence," he replied, standing tall with a flick of his tail.

Merlin shook his paw at her. "I'm warning you, Eliza, keep your mind of the task at hand. No more romantic romps."

Chapter Two

Because her contact at the University of Vienna could not meet her until the next afternoon, Eliza grabbed Merlin's portable pet carrier—a backpack—and brought him with her to the Spanish Riding School. She stood mesmerized in the grand, airy space watching the Lipizzaners as they glided gracefully through their routines. Such dancers of the equine world moved in perfect harmony with their trainers. Even Merlin took an interest as his luminous eyes scanned the arena below their gallery.

"It's just a practice. Their morning exercises," she whispered to him.

"Now these are beasts who look like even I could ride them," Merlin responded. "Not like what you made me do in Italy the last time."

He referred to an emergency at Eliza's last assignment when she made her cat tear off on a horse to look for help.

She met with Lukas Berger on the first level. He was a

The Spanish Riding School Incident

toned middle-aged man with close-cropped head of greying hair.

"Could you show us around?" Eliza begged.

"Certainly. Now keep in mind I cannot give you lessons here. For that we have permission with a friend of mine at another location."

"I'd love that," Eliza cooed.

As they strolled further into the stables, the aroma of hay and freshly brushed horses enveloped them, mingling with the faint sound of hooves echoing against the wooden floor. Lukas led the way, gesturing towards an aged school stallion with a built forehand and muscular haunches. "This is Belissimo. He's a bit of a king but don't let his sassy attitude fool you; he's got a heart of gold and loves to perform."

Merlin, with his tail flicking curiously, responded, "A king, you say? I could show him a thing or two about royal bearings." His voice, smooth and confident, lilted through the dim light.

"Really? A royal cat offering lessons to a horse? That sounds like an affair worthy of a ballad!" Lukas chuckled, leaning over the stall to get a closer look at the horse, who nickered softly in response.

They continued down the row, where Lukas introduced them to a magnificent stallion with a shimmering coat. "This is Theo. He's a workhorse and a showstopper. You should see him in the ring during competitions."

Merlin observed closely, squinting as if sizing up Theo. "He seems like a good sport. I might challenge him to a friendly round later."

"A friendly round?" Eliza teased. "You do realize you're a cat, right? You would need a saddle to even think about keeping up!"

"Ah, but my dear human, you underestimate the prowess of a magical creature." Merlin winked, then added, "Now, if I had a saddle, that would be a different story!"

With every new horse, Lukas shared anecdotes filled with charm and humor, drawing Eliza and Merlin deeper into the world of equestrian culture. He discussed their unique personalities. As they walked by a massive, well organized tack room, Eliza swooned. "So beautiful," she murmured.

They reached the final stall, where a gentle white gelding stood, looking curiously at his visitors. "And this is Snowflake," Lukas said, his voice softening. "He's calm and wise beyond his years. A perfect choice for anyone new to riding. We start our beginner inductees on him."

. . .

The Spanish Riding School Incident

"He looks like he would be quite agreeable," Eliza remarked, stepping closer. "What do you think, Merlin? Would you ride on a horse like that?"

Merlin puffed out his chest. "Of course! I would charm him into letting me direct him."

"You're quite the character, Merlin," Lukas grinned. "I must admit, I've never met a cat like you. How would you feel about a private riding lesson?"

Merlin guffawed.

"We've come to the end of our tour." Lukas pressed a folded piece of paper into Eliza's hand. "These are the details for how to get to the estate. An Uber should suffice. When would you like to begin?"

Eliza rocked back on her heels. "I need to see what the director at the University says first. Can I text you?"

"Indeed!" Lukas told her.

After a small feast, Eliza and her cat settled into the cozy confines of the living room, where Eliza grabbed her sketchbook and crayons. "How about I draw some possible hats for you to wear for your grand debut?"

. . .

Merlin tilted his head, intrigued. "Hats? You mean I can adorn myself in princely attire? Perhaps a dashing cape and a crown to truly command the attention of both horse and rider? Eliza, you must whip up such an outfit for me."

"I will. You'll be pleased. After we go to the University to set up, we'll see when Lukas can meet with us, okay Merlin?"

Chapter Three

They headed to the university for Eliza's meeting with Professor Berlin. As they walked across the stately campus, Eliza could barely contain her excitement. "Professor Berlin is the leading authority on historic textiles here. I can't believe I'll be working with him to study old dye techniques!"

Merlin yawned exaggeratedly. "Yes, analyzing mud colors sounds like a delight."

Eliza smiled at her haughty cat. She checked the directions she'd been given to Professor Berlin's office. "Ah, here's the Anthropology building."

They climbed two flights of stairs crowded with students to a hallway lined with offices. Eliza checked the plaques next to the doors until she found one labeled "Prof. Dr. H.E.R. Berlin." She took a breath to compose herself and knocked firmly.

"Herein!" a reedy voice called out. Eliza opened the door to reveal an office in utter disarray, with teetering stacks of books and papers covering every surface. A spidery man with wild grey hair and a crooked bowtie blinked at them owlishly through thick glasses.

"Professor Berlin? I'm Eliza Bennett, we spoke over email about meeting today to discuss historic textiles."

"Of course, Fräulein Bennett, forgive my clutter," Professor Berlin said distractedly, shuffling a pile of books off a chair so she could sit. As he did so, a cloud of dust erupted into the air, causing Merlin to let out an indignant sneeze.

"Bless you, Merlin," Eliza said.

"Thank you, my dear human."

The professor stopped in his tracks. "I apologize, I tend to get lost in my research and forget the cleaning," Professor Berlin said. He peered interestedly at Merlin. "And who is this fellow?"

"This is my cat, Merlin. I hope you don't mind if he sits in while we talk," Eliza said.

Professor Berlin smiled delightedly. "Of course not! I always say one can never have enough fuzzy creatures around. Especially talking ones, yes?" He winked at Merlin, who sat up primly.

"Well, at least someone here recognizes my intellectual contributions," Merlin proclaimed loftily.

Professor Berlin chuckled. "Ah, a cat of discerning taste and opinion, *sehr gut*! I can see we shall get along splendidly."

He and Eliza quickly fell into an animated discussion about dye sources used in historical Central European textiles. Professor Berlin brought out samples of old wool and linen swatches, pointing out subtle variances in color hue and saturation.

"Now this blue, you see how it has a slight grey undertone? That indicates likely use of indigo as the dye source.

The Spanish Riding School Incident

But this one has a more vibrant purple-blue. That shade came from rare woad plants."

As they examined the samples, Merlin interjected his thoughts frequently. "No, no, that green is clearly not Celtic in origin, it lacks the subtle olive undertones..." and "My dear professor, surely that red is not madder but rather cochineal, note the slight orange cast."

Professor Berlin welcomed Merlin's perspectives, scribbling notes eagerly. "Your cat has a remarkable eye! I may have been mistaken about the origin of that green, the olive tones do indicate Celtic dyes."

After an invigorating couple of hours, Professor Berlin sat back with satisfaction. "My friends, this has been most illuminating. Your knowledge of historical textiles is impressive. And Merlin, your insights are unparalleled. You must join us when we venture into the Vienna Woods to gather dye samples."

Merlin preened at the praise. "Well, I do take color quite seriously. One's appearance is so important, after all."

Eliza had to hide her smile at Merlin's vanity, plus she was thrilled.

The professor leaned forward. "But first, if you have time this evening, join me for a reception at the faculty club to meet my colleagues. I would love to show you off, I mean, introduce them to your impressive knowledge."

Eliza smiled, touched by the professor's enthusiasm. "We would be delighted to attend." Merlin flicked his tail happily at the invitation.

That evening, Eliza selected a smart blazer and skirt, while Merlin groomed his whiskers to perfection. "One does wish to make the proper impression," he declared.

At the reception, Professor Berlin proudly introduced

Eliza and Merlin to his fellow scholars. Merlin immediately jumped into intellectual debates with the professors.

"You think flax was the primary medieval fiber? My good man, have you examined the weave patterns in Flemish tapestries? Clearly wool was dominant."

The professor Merlin was addressing stroked his beard thoughtfully. "Your point is well-taken. Perhaps I should review the evidence."

Eliza discussed dye techniques with the faculty, but felt herself drawn again and again to a dark, sardonic man who hung at the edge of the room. At last she approached him. "Hello, I don't think we've met. I'm Eliza Bennett."

He shook her hand reluctantly. "Dr. Johann Schwarzkopf, Chemistry department." His eyes narrowed at Merlin winding between her ankles. "I see you've brought a cat. How charming." His tone indicated he found it anything but.

Merlin's fur bristled at the veiled insult. "My good sir, I am no mere cat, but a scholar of refinement and discernment. You would do well to reconsider your biases."

Dr. Schwarzkopf raised an eyebrow contemptuously. "Well, Miss Bennett, when you tire of traveling with a novelty pet, perhaps you would care to collaborate with a serious academic." He stalked off without waiting for her reply.

Eliza frowned, but just then Professor Berlin bustled over. "Come, come! We are retiring to a private bar for even more drinks and conversation."

There, a group of professors gathered around Merlin, clearly fascinated by his eloquence. "We have never heard a cat speak so intelligently on Baroque tapestry weaving," one said. Even Dr. Schwarzkopf reluctantly joined the circle, though his expression remained sour.

The Spanish Riding School Incident

Late into the night, the gathering discussed history and philosophy. Eliza was having trouble keeping her eyes open when at last the professors bid them goodnight.

Back at the apartment, Merlin curled up smugly on his pillow. "Well, that was most stimulating! Did you hear Professor Heinrich compare my intellect to Montesquieu's? I knew I would liven up that dreary reception."

Eliza laughed and stroked his back. "Yes, you were the life of the party. Even Dr. Schwarzkopf, that old coot, paid attention once you started lecturing on oxidation levels in lichen dyes." Merlin purred proudly in reply as Eliza turned out the light.

Chapter Four

As dawn's first light began to filter through the dense canopy of trees, Eliza, Merlin, and Professor Berlin stepped into the vibrant, dew-kissed underbrush of the Vienna woods. Eliza's thick leather boots squelched softly as they penetrated the rich, damp earth, sending a few startled woodland creatures scrambling into the thickets. Merlin, ever the curious observer, trotted beside her, his orange fur a striking splash against the lush greens surrounding them.

"Stay close, Eliza," Professor Berlin called, his eyes darting over the ground with focused enthusiasm. He used a tall staff to help him walk and clung tightly to it. Eliza noticed he did stand up straighter with the cane.

"The mushrooms like to play hide and seek among the shadows. Look for the ones that wrinkle up like old men's knuckles! Of course that excludes me." His voice was a melodious mix of authority and excitement, and Eliza grinned at the odd imagery he conjured.

The Spanish Riding School Incident

. . .

Eliza knelt, her fingers brushing through the cool soil, a flicker of something white catching her eye beneath a sprawling fern. "Look, Professor!" she exclaimed, pointing to a cluster of delicate mushrooms peeking out modestly from their leafy blanket. "Could these be the wood blewit?"

Taking on a scholar's gravity, Professor Berlin approached, his eyes concentrating as he inspected her find. "Ah, yes! Quite promising indeed." He inserted his spade gently into the earth, coaxing the mushrooms from their home. "But let's not disturb them too recklessly. Remember, for every one we collect, there are countless more lessons to learn from the ecosystem itself."

Merlin wandered a few paces away, peering at a curious patch of fungi with a richly textured cap. "Oh, what's this one?" he called, half-amused. "I hope it doesn't bite!"

"It's not just a mushroom, my whiskered friend, it's a false chanterelle," the professor explained, chuckling at the cat. "Edible but lacking the flavor one hopes for—like a thief with poor taste."

As the trio moved deeper into the woods, the air thickened with the earthy scent of damp leaves and the sweet whisper of decay—nature's own perfume. Organic life buzzed all around them: a symphony of rustling leaves, distant birds, and the gentle thrum of a brook nearby. Eliza felt invigorated, as if the forest were weaving magic into her very soul.

Merlin took on the role of a self-appointed scout, leaping between tree roots, his tail twitching excitedly. "Over here! I think I've found a treasure!" he exclaimed, standing dramatically at the base of a grand oak, like a feline explorer revealing a new world.

Eliza laughed, brushing strands of hair from her forehead as she joined him. Before them lay a bed of golden chanterelles, their color radiant in the filtered sunlight. "You've outdone yourself, Merlin!" she said, her heart swelling with pride.

"Of course! I have an eye for the exquisite," Merlin purred, puffing out his chest. "All in a day's work for a cat with a nose for justice—and gourmet cuisine!"

"But the royal purple, professor! Where might we find those kinds of mushrooms?" Eliza asked.
"Ah, there are several types that suffice for that. Come with me."
He led them to a small outcropping of rock and pointed to the base where several logs lay in a rotting heap. Growing like plates along the bark were several specimens of fungi.
Eliza's eyes lit up. "My goodness!"
He smiled. "Hapalopilus nidulans." Then he glanced at

The Spanish Riding School Incident

his watch. "Oh. I need to get back to teach. Come along, Merlin! Let's gather some quick."

Professor Berlin knelt beside Eliza, cradling a few of the glistening fungi in his hands. "With these, we shall complete our collection, and I'll show you how to extract the dyes. I'll save these. Perhaps this evening? It seems today shall be fruitful!" His eyes sparkled with the thrill of academic pursuit.

Chapter Five

Eliza and Merlin bade the professor goodbye as he dropped them off. She watched as his old Volvo belched down the street. "He's a smart man," she said to Merlin, turning and shading her eyes from the morning sun.

"Indeed. Do we have time for breakfast before our next outing?"

"You'll have to eat dried," she warned him.

"Drats."

"Let's go upstairs so I can change and call an Uber."

Lukas Berger met Eliza and Merlin at the front gate of a gigantic estate. The gate had a royal crest on it and a massive raised relief metal designed that would rival Versailles. Eliza saw off to the right were the stables and a large riding arena.

. . .

The Spanish Riding School Incident

"I'm so pleased you made it," the older teacher crooned as he pressed a button to let them in. "Let's walk down this path."

Lukas put Eliza through her paces on a school horse named Bixo. While she rode, an extremely handsome 30-year-old man came out of the massive main house.

"Ah, Max. You've decided to join us," Lukas said. "Eliza Bennett, meet Max Muller.

Merlin jumped onto a bench near Max.

"That's her cat, Merlin," Lukas said.

"Pleased to meet you," Merlin said, taking a small bow.

Eliza was on a lunge line going at a trot around her new instructor. Each time Max came into view, she wanted to have Lukas stop the action. The man was as gorgeous as a Greek god. Her heart rate accelerated and she knew it wasn't just from the riding.

Merlin, with his ability to perceive humans' heart rates, knew instantly his owner was attracted to this upscale man.

"Not again," he grumbled to himself softly from his perch.

Max stood ringside taking in the scene.

"Is her girth tightened enough?" he asked Lukas.

Lukas slowed Bixo. "Good eye. Actually, it's not."

Max slipped under the rail and approached Eliza. "Here, I'll do it. Stay where you are, Lukas."

Max winked at Eliza. "Bixo has this ole trick down pat.

He always bloats up when we first put a saddle on him. I know his ways." He gently placed a hand on the calf of her boot and gave her leg a pat. "You're all good now."

Eliza's leg felt as if it had turned into fire where Max touched her.

Merlin watched everything with a jaundiced eye. "Oh jeez. She's in love again," he muttered out loud to nobody in particular.

Max flashed Eliza a broad smile and returned to his post.

"We will resume where we left off," Lukas told Eliza. "Now hold onto the strap and engage your core. Lean back with a tightened torso and we'll pick up the canter. Bixo has a nice steady one."

"Weeeeee!" Eliza chortled as the trained horse lifted into a smooth canter.

Max glanced at Merlin. "How long has she been riding?"

"Several years. But she doesn't own a horse of her own."

"I see."

Lukas touched the houndstooth hat Merlin proudly wore.

"This makes you look like Sherlock Holmes," he told the cat.

"Posh! This ole hat. Eliza zipped it out for me overnight. She likes a well-dressed man."

. . .

The Spanish Riding School Incident

Their banter continued, light-hearted and energetic, while Max remained fixed on Eliza, his expression shifting to one of genuine intrigue. He stepped forward, stroking Merlin's back. "So, is riding all she does? Or do you two have a job in the States?" he asked.

"She's a professor, but I'm the brains of the operation."

"Wow, you're really laying it on, huh?" Max said.

Merlin waved a paw dismissively. "Eliza's a complicated woman, Max. You might be in over your head here."

"Oh?" Max replied, a glint of mischief in his eyes. "Complicated can be fascinating. I thrive on a challenge." The way he looked at her, as if she were the only one that mattered in that moment, sent her heart racing.

Lukas rolled his eyes with an exasperated grin. "Let's not scare her away on the first day," he joked. "Maybe this time we can convince Merlin to try some riding."

"No thanks!" Merlin exclaimed, throwing his paws wildly in the air. "I prefer my pads on the ground. These horses are completely out of control!"

"Merlin, it's just a horse," Eliza called teasingly as she prepared again for the next transition. "You could at least try a walk!"

. . .

With the playful conversation swirling around them, the atmosphere felt electric. Just as she set her eyes straight ahead, a shadow flickered in the upper turret of the house. Eliza's focus broke momentarily. She glanced upward to see the woman with striking features watching intently. "Who's that?" she asked, pulling back on the reins.

"That's Sophia, my sister," Max said, glancing up as well. His tone shifted, revealing a hint of annoyance. "She likes to play the audience, especially when there are guests around."

Merlin raised an eyebrow. "She doesn't look like she enjoys the show very much," he said, noticing the set of her frown.

"Oh, she's judging," Max said with a smirk. "It's kind of her thing. Just give her a moment, she might like it."

"That's not very assuring," Merlin replied.

Eliza laughed, but there was an unpredictable undercurrent in Max's voice that caught her attention. "Well, I'd hate to distract her from her judging," she said, keeping her face forward like Lukas had told her to do.

"Just keep being amazing," Max encouraged softly, his voice

The Spanish Riding School Incident

low and earnest—just loud enough for everyone to hear. "That'll definitely catch her eye."

Eliza nodded. "Always," she said with a wink before turning to Lukas.

"Can we do some more canter? I need the practice."

"You do better than my sister," he called out over the arena. "She refuses to ever go faster than a trot."

Lukas shook his head. "Well, she did have that accident...."

As the lesson came to an end, Eliza dismounted, a rush of giddiness filled her veins. "So, what do you do for fun around here besides watching the local horse show?" she asked Max.

"Oh, there's plenty. We have a small gallery in the west wing with my mother's collection of modern art which is used for functions. Then there are movie nights by the pool, and you can even explore the gardens."

"I might have to check out that gallery, then," Eliza said, intrigued. "Art is another one of my passions."

"Perhaps I should give you a personal tour," Max suggested, his voice dipping into a conspiratorial tone. "I could use the company."

. . .

Lukas raised an eyebrow, but he couldn't hide his own smile. "Careful, Max. Don't get too distracted from your sister's watchful eye. I know how she loves to stir the pot."

"You have no idea," Max replied, shaking his head with amusement. "But the more she watches, the more I want to have some fun."

Eliza felt a glow beneath her skin as she caught Max's eye again. The allure of the opulent estate, mixed with the thrill of the ride, shaped a bond that felt instant yet mysterious.

"Speaking of fun," Lukas interrupted, "how about we all get something to drink? There's a little café nearby that serves the best coffee."

"I'm in! I could use a break," Eliza responded, her spirits undimmed.

"Count me in too. I need a distraction," Max said, glancing once more at the distant figure in the window.

As they turned toward the path leading to the café, Eliza caught a glimpse of Sophia before the curtain in the turret fluttered shut. Something about the encounter left a lingering curiosity in her mind, but as she began to walk alongside Max, she pushed those thoughts aside for now.

The Spanish Riding School Incident

. . .

"So, what's the best way to drink coffee here?" Eliza asked, teasingly nudging Max with her shoulder.

"We like melange which you know as cappuccino."

Chapter Six

Eliza's research into the mycological wonders of Vienna's forests was proving to be more fascinating than she had ever anticipated. The mushrooms she discovered were not only diverse in their species but also held a rich history in the art of fabric dyeing. She spent her days poring over ancient texts at the Vienna National Library and some afternoons trekking through the lush underbrush, Merlin padding silently beside her.

Professor Berlin showed her how he applied heat to the mushrooms to extract the right hues. She began to visit his lab more frequently.

Despite her busy schedule, Eliza found herself eagerly anticipating her lessons with Lukas. At least they shared a connection over their love of horses. He proved to be a skilled instructor. Merlin could tell, though, that the real reason she liked taking so many lessons was it gave her a chance to visit the Muller estate.

. . .

The Spanish Riding School Incident

Finally, one day Max sauntered out and suggested the three of them go on a small trail ride around the estate and then have dinner. Lukas begged off. He had a performance that evening. Max looked at Eliza. "And you?"

"I'd love to. As long as I can carry Merlin with me. He's never done so much walking in all his life. Isn't that right, pumpkin?"

Merlin gave a half sneer. "I mean, I could keep up but hitchhiking would be so much easier on my delicate little toes."

The ride extended into the twilight hours, with Max showing the extensive grounds. Eliza was almost lulled to sleep by Bixo's strong steady walk and their bodies moving in harmony with the powerful animals beneath them.

Merlin, however, was not nearly as enamored with Max. "I don't trust him, Eliza," Merlin grumbled, his green eyes narrowing after Max helped Eliza dismount and led the horses back to their barn. "There's something about him that sets my whiskers on edge."

"Oh, Merlin, not this again," Eliza replied brushing off her riding pants. "You're just jealous that I'm spending time with someone other than you."

Merlin huffed in response, his tail flicking with irritation. "Jealousy has nothing to do with it. I'm concerned for your safety. You're getting too close to this rich world, to this man. It's clouding your judgment."

. . .

Eliza laughed off Merlin's concerns, but the cat's words lingered in the back of her mind that evening.

Max took them into the main house by way of the eight-car garage.

"Oh my," Eliza exclaimed. "So many cars."

"My parents like to collect them," Max explained.

"Where are your parents?"

"Traveling. But no matter. I had our cook make us something special."

Eliza felt herself truly lost in the romance of it all.

Once inside the house, Max rang a small dinner bell and waited. Eliza and Merlin stood in a dining hall with twenty-two foot high ceilings.

Max frowned. "We're waiting on her highness."

They heard the whirl of an elevator, then the sound of the doors as they opened.

"Wow, this house has everything," Merlin whispered to Eliza.

"Sophia, meet our guests. You've been watching all of their lessons, anyway," Max said as a tall, thin blond woman entered the room.

Eliza watched the woman walk. She had a bad limp and wore a long dress.

"Hello," Sophia said. "You look nice out there."

"Thank you," Eliza responded.

"It's difficult for me to ride any more," Sophia stated. Then she took her hand and pounded it into her thigh. A dull, hollow sound echoed throughout the room.

The Spanish Riding School Incident

"That's enough," Max commanded.

Eliza exchanged a worried glance with Merlin.

Max was eager to impress his new acquisition, Eliza. He opened a bottle of light red wine as the cook began to bring out the food.

Merlin popped open his eyes at the display of pumpkin soup, wiener schnitzel and potato salad.

Sophia, his bitter sister, lingered at his side, clearly envious of Eliza's presence.

The aroma of freshly baked bread and grilled meats wafted through the air as they all sat down at the table. Max poured some wine for each guest, eager to start the night off on a good note.

"This wine is splendid," Eliza remarked, taking a sip from her glass. "Where did you manage to find it?"

"Oh, this?" Max smiled, pleased with her compliment. "I acquired it on one of my trips to a local vineyard. Not many know about this vintage. It's quite rare."

Sophia rolled her eyes, clearly unimpressed. "Well, I hope it doesn't make you too sleepy, Max. We have plans for tonight," she said, shooting a pointed look Eliza's way.

. . .

Merlin jumped onto his spot at the table, meowing for Eliza's attention. She giggled and picked him up, petting his soft fur.

"I think Merlin wants to stay up late too, Sophia," she said gently, setting the cat back down on his chair. "He doesn't seem too fond of the idea of us spending the evening together."

Max grinned, patting Eliza's hand under the table. "Oh, don't worry about old Sophia. She's just jealous because she can't have some fun herself. Besides, you're starting to know how I feel about you, Eliza."

He winked at Eliza taking another sip of wine. Sophia scoffed, turning her attention back to her food. But Eliza smiled softly, feeling warmth spread through her chest. This was the kind of feeling she hadn't experienced in a while.

They all continued to enjoy the meal, engrossed in conversation and each other's company. As the night wore on and the wine continued to flow, Max looked at Eliza with an unspoken question in his eyes. She returned his gaze, a knowing smile tugging at her lips.

The wine flowed as Max kept initiating toasts. The night wore on, Sophia became less able to maintain her faux pleasantries.

"Oh, that reminds me," Eliza chimed in suddenly, cutting through the tension in the room. "Merlin and I have a little performance planned for you all. It's just a small little something we've been working on."

Sophia grunted, an arrogant smirk on her lips, as she poured another glass of wine for herself. "Really, Eliza? You think you can entertain us? As if we haven't seen enough from you already." The mockery in her voice was unmistakable, but Eliza brushed it off, smiling sweetly at the man instead who had quickly become her adoring fan.

"Yes, Sophia, I do believe we can," she replied coolly, her gaze sharp and determined to prove her wrong despite her sweet exterior. The duo proceeded with their act, something they had practiced many times over the past few weeks.

Merlin, perched on the edge of the side table, following Eliza's every command, a living puppet at her fingertips. They danced together, the cat jumping and prancing across the table while Eliza performed a graceful dance of her own while humming a tune. Max and the bitter Sophia, watched in awe as Merlin performed leaps and flips.

"I didn't know the old boy had it in him," Max said.

"Well, first off I'm not old."

. . .

"You're awfully fluffy and surprisingly agile," Sophia noted.

"Fluffy or fat, madame?" Merlin interjected. "I'll have your know I'm in better shape than anyone in this room."

But as the wine started to take effect, Eliza became increasingly aware of Merlin's unease. The cat sensed her desire for Max, and while he understood Eliza's attraction to the man with the lavish estate, he also felt something else —a sense of protective instinct as if Eliza wanting to be with Max wasn't right.

"Okay, Eliza," Merlin would whisper in a quiet voice, his ears twitching ever so slightly. "You've gotten your audience in awe and made Max's sister eat her own jealousy. Time to call it a night."

Perhaps Merlin was right. She needed to tread carefully with Max. But something about Max's eyes and lips made her feel like she could share her secrets with him without being judged.

"Merlin, darling, you worry too much," she whispered back to him. "Max is just a gentleman who happens to be nice to me. Besides, I haven't felt this way in a long time. It's wonderful. But I do promise you, I won't do anything you don't like."

. . .

The Spanish Riding School Incident

Following this, Eliza stood from her chair, gracefully adjusting her dress to the side. She was acutely aware of the attention her decision would bring. But Max, sensing that Eliza was getting ready to say her goodbyes, quietly intervened.

"My dear, please do not leave so soon," Max said in a hushed voice, his eyes pleading with Eliza. He placed a gentle hand on her arm. "There's so much more to tell you about this wonderful place, about me."

Merlin watched with displeasure, his little heart thumping hard against his ribs. He didn't trust Max completely and he knew Eliza could get hurt if she wasn't careful. But despite this, he remained quiet, merely watching as Eliza engaged with Max on a different note. They continued to chat, laugh and sip their wine, all under the soft glow of the candles and the sparkle of the starry night beyond the window.

Sophia was clearly fuming. Her fists clenched, her lips pursed tight, her eyes on Max and Eliza all the time, burning with envy. Not because of Max, but maybe because of Eliza's easy charm and beauty. It was unnerving for her and she knew she couldn't let Eliza stay.

Sophia cleared her throat, drawing attention to herself.

. . .

"It's quite lovely to see Merlin being so attached to you, Eliza." She said, her tone light and casual, but her eyes narrowed. "But I bet he's much fonder of his usual treats. The chef surely prepared something special for him, don't you agree Max?"

Max looked up from where he was locked with Eliza in conversation. He blinked a couple of times, then nodded. "Of course," he said, turning to the chef. "Bring out Merlin's treats. He ought to be spoiled a little more, don't you think?"

Sophia smiled, relaxing slightly as the conversation moved towards a less troubling topic. Merlin, taking this as a cue, launched into a detailed narration of his last visit to the vet, much to everyone's amusement. Max kept subtly trying to recapture Eliza's attention, but the cat persistently blocked every attempt, leading to various interesting events that kept each of them on their toes.

Sophia's plan had backfired spectacularly. As she left the dining room to confront the chef about Merlin's treats, Max became bolder in his pursuit of Eliza. He peppered her with praise and charm. But it wasn't until she gladly took a piece of his favorite cake, his actions taking on a more intimate nature, that he finally felt confident enough to make his move.

"Max, do you ever stop to think that you might be overselling yourself?" Sophia's voice cut through the warm

The Spanish Riding School Incident

air as she reentered the dining room, arms crossed defiantly. She shot a quick glance at Merlin, who blinked back at her with an expression that was almost smug, as if he were entertained by the unfolding drama.

Eliza giggled, clearly enjoying the way Max leaned closer, his intensity growing. "Oh, come on, Sophia! Max has such fascinating stories. They're like little windows into a world I've never seen."

"Right, fascinating!" Sophia hissed, and crossed to the table, her frustration noticeable. "Like the time you fished for mermaids in the lake, or maybe the one about how you single-handedly climbed that mountain." She rolled her eyes, struggling to keep her voice steady.

"Oh, Sophia, you know I love embellishing a little," Max replied, kicking his sister under the table, a mischievous smile playing on his lips. "But you can't deny that they're a lot more interesting than your knitting stories."

Eliza chuckled again, her eyes sparkling with mischief. "Knitting stories? Now I'm intrigued! Maybe I should take lessons. Right, Merlin?" She affectionately scratched the cat behind the ears, and the feline let out a soft purr that seemed to echo her sentiments. "You do know I'm a textile scientist, don't you?"

. . .

Max interjected, feigning exasperation but fighting back laughter. "Be careful, Eliza will have you knitting sweaters for Merlin next."

Max leaned even closer to Merlin, his tone suddenly dropping to a conspiratorial whisper. "I actually think it would be quite charming to see you with a regal-looking scarf, all snug like the winter's first snow."

Sophia straight-lined her lips, seething slightly. "You've got to be kidding me. Really? A scarf? What's next, a matching hat?"

Eliza, clearly more amused than annoyed, shot Sophia a teasing grin. "That doesn't sound bad at all. I'd get to spend more time with both of you!"

"Oh, joy," Sophia muttered, searching frantically for a way to break this charming spell her brother had cast. "But don't you think it's getting a bit ridiculous?"

Max turned to Eliza, feigning contemplation. "And yet, nothing brings us together like cake, does it? Perhaps it is a secret ingredient to win your heart." He offered Eliza a delicate slice from the plate, feeding it to her with his fork.

Sophia watched as Eliza accepted the piece with a smile, their fingers brushing ever so slightly—and Merlin, perched regally nearby, seemed to know this was just the start of the evening's unfolding drama.

Chapter Seven

The grand chandelier cast a warm glow across the ornate ceiling of Max's Viennese manor. Candlelight danced across Eliza's porcelain skin as she gazed at her host, her eyes gleaming with intrigue.

"You know, Eliza, it's not often I meet a woman as brilliant as you." Max flashed her a roguish grin, his chiseled jawline highlighted by the flickering flames.

Eliza blushed, feeling her pulse quicken. "Well, Max, I could say the same about you."

Max's eyes smoldered with unspoken desire as they roamed Eliza's voluptuous figure.

The two flirted shamelessly exchanging playful banter and lingering looks. At the dinner table, the attraction had simmered, charged with sexual tension. Eliza's Merlin observed from under the table, his whiskers twitching with resentment.

The Spanish Riding School Incident

After the dessert, Max stood abruptly. "Excuse me, dear Merlin, but I find myself needing a breath of fresh air."

Merlin narrowed his eyes.

Max offered Eliza his arm. "Allow me to escort you to the garden." She accepted gracefully, ignited by anticipation.

Crisp night air filled Eliza's lungs as they strolled through flawlessly manicured hedges. Moonlight spilled over rippling ponds and ornate statues. But Eliza only had eyes for Max. He led her to a secluded gazebo draped in twinkling fairy lights, tilting her chin upward to face him.

"So tell me Eliza," he breathed, "have you ever been kissed in the moonlight?"

"I don't think so," Eliza whispered, trembling under his smoldering stare.

"Bullshit," Merlin snarled in a low growl.

Max closed the remaining distance between them, claiming Eliza's mouth in a fierce, passionate kiss. She melted against him, losing herself in his intoxicating embrace. His tongue delved past her parted lips, stroking sensually against hers. Eliza moaned softly, desire raging through her veins.

Max swept Eliza into his powerful arms, carrying her bridal-style back towards the manor. "Allow me to show you to my private chambers," he murmured against her neck.

"Yes...please..." Eliza whimpered breathlessly, surrendering to him.

Merlin followed and kept batting at the cuff of Max's pants.

. . .

Max kicked open the heavy oak door, laying Eliza down on a plush king-sized bed. The room was decadent, all rich mahogany furnishings and plush crimson velvet, all man cave. He sank down beside her, trailing hot kisses along her jawline. Eliza arched into him, her breasts heaving with need.

Eliza's fingers raked through his dark hair, pulling him closer.

Merlin hopped onto the bed.

"Listen kids, you need to stop this."

Eliza sat up and stared pointedly at the floor. "Get down," she commanded.

"No."

"My god, Eliza," Max rumbled, his own lust consuming him. "Will you forget about the cat?"

There was a pounding at the door.

"Jesus," Max grumbled.

"The maid is finished with your ironing," Sophia called from the hallway.

. . .

The Spanish Riding School Incident

"Leave us alone."

Merlin gave a final hiss then bolted out of the room when Sophia cracked open the door to throw the shirts onto Max's floor. Neither Eliza nor Max noticed this.

"Don't mind him," Eliza murmured. "Merlin's an incorrigible voyeur."

Eliza peered up at Max through hooded lashes. "Honestly, I don't care if Merlin watches the whole show. In fact, I'd very much like a Part Two later—if you're up for it." Eliza trailed a fingertip teasingly down Max's sweat-slicked chest.

Meanwhile Merlin began prowling the wide, lavish corridors, illuminated by sconces. His whiskers twitched with curiosity. The air was thick with an inexplicable quiet, interspersed with the occasional creak of the ancient floorboards beneath his heavy paws.

With an effortless leap, the cat ascended the sweeping staircase, his agile form fluid and graceful. Each step felt instinctual, his feline nature guided him towards the mysteries that lay above. He paused at the top. With perked ears he regarded the dimly lit hallway. Instinctively, he felt the pull of Sophia's bedroom, a sanctuary of her own creation that promised intrigue.

Quiet as a whisper, Merlin padded down the corridor, his tail flicking attentively. He nudged the door ajar with his paw, slipping into the room unseen. What greeted him was a striking contrast to the expected clutter of a young woman's space; it was remarkably organized, a testament to Sophia's deliberate nature. The scent of fresh linen mixed with a faint hint of lavender wafted through the air, speaking of hours spent perfecting her world.

Merlin's golden gaze swept the room, landing immediately on an impressive array of weights lined up against one wall. An entire gym in the heart of a mansion! He mused inwardly, intrigued by the iron and metal, the distinct shapes gleaming under the flickering light. There were dumbbells of various sizes, kettlebells, and even a bench press—tools of strength and discipline, each bearing the scuffs and scars of countless workouts.

But it wasn't the gym that commanded Merlin's attention most; it was the alluring glint of steel further into the room. He padded closer. There, displayed with care, was an impressive collection of knives nestled within a dark wood case. Each blade glistened invitingly, some sharp enough to catch the light and dance with reflections. It was a collection that spoke to artistry as much as functionality—each weapon, an extension of will.

Merlin hopped onto a nearby dresser, his curiosity heightened. He pawed at the air, as if to summon a breeze to stir the intricate patterns engraved on the knives' handles. The craftsmanship was exquisite, ranging from ornate

The Spanish Riding School Incident

designs to sleek, modern edges. His feline instincts told him that while they were beautiful, they held a far more sinister purpose when wielded in skilled hands.

A flicker of movement caught his attention, drawing his gaze to a corner of the room where a target practice setup stood. A circular target, brilliantly painted in concentric rings, sprawled against the wall. A small stack of knives lay precariously close, each perfectly balanced and sharp-edged. Sophia's prowess here was unmistakable—she seemed to command her tools with a confidence that intrigued even the wary Merlin.

He envisioned Sophia deftly stepping back, a steadfast stance as she flung each knife with unwavering focus. A true warrior in every sense.

As he mused, a creak broke through the silence. Merlin froze, his senses honing in on any sign of movement. The door swung open slightly, and Sophia herself entered the room, sweat glistening on her brow, a towel slung casually around her shoulders. Her athletic wear clung to her form, hinting at her recent exertions.

"Well, well, what do we have here?" Sophia's voice rang out, a mixture of surprise and amusement as she spotted Merlin perched on the dresser and hobbled over.

His iridescent eyes met hers, and in that instant, there was a palpable connection—a shared understanding between the enigmatic cat and the spirited woman. "Just your average inquisitive feline," Merlin said. His demeanor as regal as ever.

Sophia laughed, the sound rich and musical, a moment of levity breaking the intensity of the masked warrior that lingered within her. She walked over to the weights and began arranging them, her movements fluid, a ballet of strength and grace. "You've got a good eye, Merlin. I suppose you're curious about my collection."

Merlin hopped down from the dresser, deciding to engage. He wound around her ankles, an artful display meant to convey both admiration and camaraderie. As she bent to her task, he took a moment to explore further, nudging a loose knife with his paw, making it sway slightly.

"Training keeps me sharp, in more ways than one."

Sophia's laughter faded, and as if a switch had been flipped, her demeanor shifted. A shadow crossed her face, and her smile twisted into something that made Merlin's fur bristle —the change was instantaneous, chilling the air around them.

"So, you think you're up for more than just a little practice, hmm?" she asked, her voice tinged with a dark curiosity that twisted like the blade in his paws. The light in her eyes flickered, revealing an intensity that sent a jolt of unease through the normally confident feline.

Merlin instinctively stepped back, his gaze darting to the door, suddenly aware of his surroundings. The imposing walls of the room felt closer, the weight of her now sinister aura pressing against him like a suffocating cloak. "Maybe... maybe it's best for me to—" he started, his voice trailing.

Her eyes glinted with a predatory focus. "Not so fast, my little companion. We have a connection now, don't we?" She leaned in closer, her gaze unyielding. "There are certain things I need from you—much more than just practice tips."

The knife in Merlin's paws suddenly felt too heavy, a reminder of the lethal skill she had honed. He could imagine how easily those exquisite blades could draw blood. "That was a joke, right?" he attempted, maintaining a facade of nonchalance though his heart pumped beneath his orange fur.

"No joke," she replied, her voice low and commanding, each word dripping with a sinister excitement. "The world out there is full of shadows, Merlin. And I have plans—plans that require more than just ordinary strength. I need someone who can tread where most dare not."

. . .

Merlin's instincts screamed at him to retreat, his body tensing as he fought the urge to bolt. This was no longer a realm of friendly sparring; it had morphed into something darker and far more dangerous. A cat like him didn't belong within the web of Sophia's ambitions—this was no mere workout regime, but a descent into something far more treacherous.

He glanced back towards the door, breath quickening as he imagined the countless shadows of the mansion hiding even darker secrets. "I think I've had enough for tonight," he replied, his voice faltering slightly, a hint of desperation creeping in.

But Sophia stepped forward, the playfulness from moments prior replaced by an iron resolve. "You'll find, Merlin, that once you've seen the other side of strength, there's no going back. Come, let's explore the depth of your potential."

Her words were like chains, binding him to the spot, and for the first time, the thrill of adventure he had felt moments earlier evaporated, replaced by a potent fear. He couldn't shake the feeling that he was teetering on the edge of a precipice, with an invitation to plunge into the abyss.

Without another thought, Merlin sprang toward the door, his instincts kicking in full force. He had lingered too long in this twisted game, feeling the weight of her gaze on his back like a hawk watching its prey. He pushed the door open with a fervent shove, his frame darting into the corridor beyond.

"Merlin! You're being a fool!" Sophia called, her voice echoing through the halls, now imbued with an edge of impatience that dripped with an authority he had never heard before.

As he raced through the mansion, claws scratching against the polished wood floors, Merlin couldn't shake the image of her sinister smile from his mind. Shadows lurked behind every corner, whispers of danger echoing through the otherwise still air, remnants of the conversation that had morphed from camaraderie into a chilling prophecy of what awaited him if he ever returned.

He didn't stop until he reached the safety of Max's bedroom. There, he curled himself into a ball, ignoring Eliza and Max.

Very early the next morning Max brought Eliza coffee in bed. "Before we go, can you show me your mother's art collection?"

"Sure." Max led Eliza and a very sleepy Merlin to another wing of the grand house. Eliza sipped her coffee as she ogled the displays.

She noticed behind an open door a massive royal purple cloak embedded with gold thread and crystals.

. . .

"This is magnificent," she said and she fingered the fabric.
"It's been in our family for generations."
"What a nice artifact," Merlin yawned.

Chapter Eight

Eliza and Merlin made a late appearance in the gallery of the Spanish Riding School. Lukas looked up at her from the arena and gave her a big wink. He knew exactly where she spent the night. Eliza wore dark sunglasses and a high collar to hide her love bites. She even sewed a matching outfit for Merlin which left the cat embarrassed.

"I don't like this Victorian collar, Eliza."

"Shut up."
Obviously his human had a hangover, Merlin realized.

While they viewed the morning drills, they heard a loud scream. It was coming from the bottom floor. People start running to the stable area to see what had happened.

. . .

Merlin heard someone say "Oh my god, he's dead."

On their way down Eliza noticed Dr. Schwarzkorf in heavy consult with the director of the school in the stairwell.

Merlin made it to the stall first and wound through the tight crowd to see a young muscular blonde man lying in a bed of horse shavings in Snowflake's stall with his throat slit. Beside him was a crumpled purple cloak. Lukas led the horse out of the stall shaking his head.

"Why did they have to kill this farrier? I'll never know."

Someone in the crowd answered. "Well you know he made love to just about anyone and loved all the women—married or not."

Eliza, still in shock, whispered to Merlin, "This is no ordinary morning at the school." Merlin, his fur bristling, responded with an uncharacteristic soft mew.

Eliza, trying to maintain her composure, approached Dr. Schwarzkorf and the director, her voice steady despite the chaos. "What happened here?" she inquired, her dark sunglasses hiding the horror in her eyes.

Dr. Schwarzkorf, his face grim, replied, "It appears we have a murder on our hands. The farrier, a young man named Hans, was found by one of the stable hands not more than thirty minutes ago."

. . .

The Spanish Riding School Incident

The director, visibly shaken, added, "This is a disaster. We need to keep this quiet. The reputation of the school, the horses. We can't have panic spreading."

Eliza nodded sympathetically. "We'll need to cordon off the area and call the police. We must preserve the scene for evidence."

The crowd murmured with speculation. Lukas, still holding the reins of "Snowflake," interjected, "Eliza's right. And we should question everyone who had access to the stables last night. Hans may have been too popular, to put it mildly."

A stable hand, tears streaming down her face, approached Eliza. "I can't believe this happened. Hans was so full of life. He was teaching me how to shoe a horse just yesterday."

Eliza put a comforting hand on the young woman's shoulder and said gently, "We'll find out who did this. In the meantime, can you think of anyone who might have wanted to harm Hans?"

The stable hand, sniffled and replied, "I don't know. He was kind to everyone, but his personal life... it was complicated. He had a way with the horses and the ladies that sometimes caused trouble."

. . .

Merlin slipped away unnoticed for a moment, then returned brushing against Eliza's legs with a small, gold pin clutched in his mouth. Eliza bent down to examine the pin. She recognized it as the clasp of the purple cloak from the Muller mansion found next to Hans' body.

Chapter Nine

Eliza rose, clutching the pin tightly as she looked over her shoulder, where Dr. Schwarzkorf had returned to meticulously taking samples of the horse feed and hay.

Eliza gripped Lukas's arm.

"What's he doing over there?" she asked jerking her head towards the dark figure.

Lukas didn't reply at first. His gaze drifted to the male scientist, who was now engrossed in his work. "We called him in to analyze all of our hay and feed because Hans had noticed the horses' feet were crumbling. Looks like he's got his hands full."

Just then, a woman approached from the end of the long stable hall limping slightly. Eliza squinted. It was Sophia, her face a mask alternating between confusion and concern. "What happened?" Sophia called out anxiously as she approached.

"Stay back, Sophia. It's not safe right now," Lukas warned, but Eliza noticed the tension in his jaw as he watched the Muller woman.

Merlin, still on alert, growled lowly, his fur bristling. Eliza wondered, why was her cat reacting this way?

Sophia glanced at Merlin, becoming defensive. "What is it? I just came to switch out a saddle for Max. Lukas told me today was a good day to do this in between performances," she insisted, trying to keep her voice steady.

Eliza stepped forward to meet her gaze. "But you shouldn't be here right now. The house farrier, Hans... he's dead."

Sophia's eyes widened, shock flickering across her face. "Dead? No... You're mistaken!"

"I wish I were," Eliza replied, feeling the gravity of the situation weigh heavily on them all. "And this pin here? It belongs to the purple cloak from your house.

Sophia's face paled. "It's not ours!" She stammered, growing defensive. "Why are you bringing this up?"

"Eliza," Lukas interjected, his tone strained, "merely suggesting that we're all suspects until there's clarity? Isn't Hans the one who warned the director about certain horse issues?"

Dr. Schwarzkorf glanced over. "He did mention it," he said, his voice methodical. "But why would he risk that when he had no intention of ever getting involved in that sort of conversation with me?"

Eliza felt the pieces fray around her as tension hung thick in the air. As they exchanged glances, she caught a flicker of something in Sophia's eyes—an odd emotion of some sort.

"Is there something you're not telling us, Sophia?" Eliza asked. "What were you really doing here?"

"I'm just trying to help!" Sophia exclaimed, her voice rising to a near screech. "This was about Max switching saddles! Whatever Hans and your precious director were involved in doesn't have a thing to do with me! Your cat probably stole that pin from our house." She huffed. "Merlin the kleptomaniac."

Merlin growled again, and this time Eliza noticed Sophia's subtle flinch. "There's more to this than just a murder," Eliza whispered more to herself than anyone else, her instincts igniting.

Lukas caught her eye, urgency brewing in him. "We need answers, and fast. The crowd is restless. Let's not make enemies out of the people we need to question."

Eliza nodded, keeping the pin hidden in her fingers. "No jumping to conclusions just yet," she said, trying to maintain the crowd's precarious balance. "We've got to figure out who has the most to gain from Hans's death. Maybe we start right here." As the weight of Eliza's words settled, the air felt charged with suspense. Sophia raised her chin defiantly. "If there's so much suspicion, maybe I should have never come here today," she said. "What do you think you know about me?"

"I think you could be hiding something," Eliza countered, her voice steady but firm. "You were among the last to see him alive because you where supposedly down here switching out saddles."

"No, that nasty man scientist was down here when I arrived," Sophia countered.

Merlin continued his low growl, inching closer to Sophia, almost as if he sensed her distress—or something darker beneath the surface.

"I love my brother," she shot back, her voice rising again. "Max has had a tough time. I didn't even want to come. But he insisted I help him."

At that moment, Dr. Schwarzkorf stepped away from his samples, fixing their group with an analytical gaze.

"There is no trivial detail amidst such chaos," he said coolly, glancing between them. "If there's something you're holding back—be it about Hans, the horses, or yourself—this isn't the time."

Eliza seized on the doctor's words. "Exactly. Hans was concerned about the horses developing crumbling feet, but trouble in the stables is only part of the picture. He may have known something more."

Sophia's expression shifted slightly, panic flickering across her features. "He was always talking about protecting the horses. But what does that have to do with his death?"

Lukas leaned in, his voice barely above a whisper. "There were rumors about him. Something about his last affair."

Merlin chuckled. "How about multiple affairs? A man after my own heart!"

"Can it, Merlin! This is serious. Besides you haven't dated any likely candidates in years!"

Merlin gave Eliza a wink. "That's for me to know and you to find out! For all you know I have a million mini-Merlins all over the world!"

Eliza nudged him with her toe and put her fingers to her lips. "Shh. You're making up stories."

Eliza noted the change in posture from Sophia, how her jaw tightened and color drained from her cheeks. "You didn't just come here for Max, did you? You were trying to see Hans," she accused gently, hoping to draw more truth from her.

"No!" Sophia protested, but the fire in her eyes was waning. "I was here for Max's errand. That should be enough for you to understand!"

Dr. Schwarzkorf's keen perception didn't miss a beat. "What did Hans share with you, Sophia? He had his hands in a lot of places—sometimes carelessly, and it made him enemies. Did he ever mention anything to you that stood out?"

"The last time he did our horses—on our property, I might add—he mentioned that some of the horses were getting sick and..." she trailed off, a flicker of remorse flashing across her face. "And that he was worried someone might be sabotaging the feed. It's why he needed to alert the director."

Now Sophia's eyes filled with tears. "No! Hans loved the horses, he wanted to save them. It was all complicated, but it wasn't like that!"

Merlin moved closer to Eliza, bumping against her leg, sensing the emotional turmoil enveloping them all. "You may be innocent," Eliza said softly, her gaze steady on Sophia, "but you're not off the hook yet. We're all caught in this."

"The police will want every detail; we can't hide anything from them," Lukas urged. "Let's ensure we're not standing in the way of their investigation."

Chapter Ten

Merlin walked down the hall away from the murder scene and overheard a young woman on the phone in the office. It was one of the secretaries. He crouched low behind the heavy coat rack, the scent of leather and dust swirling around him. The flickering barn light cast shadows that danced along the shelves, creating a perfect concealment for the feline observer. He pricked his ears, listening intently to the hushed tones of the secretary just beyond the threshold.

"Honestly, he had it coming," the secretary whispered, her voice laden with a mix of vindication and malice. "Hans was always up to no good—running around with everyone's spouse like it was a game. They called him Hans of the Many Hands for good reason. You think the police will turn a blind eye to his past? Not a chance."

Merlin hunkered down as she continued. "I heard he was even warning the chemist about the food. Said he thought the grain was tainted somehow. But I think it's global warming's fault. Who knows—maybe that's why he ended up dead? People have a way of silencing the ones who get too close to the truth."

She placed her hands on her hips, glancing furtively down the corridor as if she feared being overheard. "But the food provider's been losing out ever since Hans gave him a heads-up. No wonder he was so eager to have the chemist in town."

Suddenly, Merlin's ears twitched as the unmistakable sound of heels clicking sharply against the wooden floor echoed from behind. He peered cautiously around the rack to see Sophia, her face a stormy sea of fury. She stormed toward Eliza, who stood casually by the open door, chatting amiably with Lukas.

"Stay away from my brother, Eliza!" Sophia's voice sliced through the air like a knife. Lukas frowned and stepped between the two women, attempting to smooth the tension.

"Sophia, really? You don't mean—"

"I do mean it!" she hissed, her icy glare fixed on Eliza. "You've waltzed in here, as if this is a playground, while you've got no idea what kind of family dynamics you're messing with!"

Eliza tilted her head in confusion, arms crossing defensively over her chest. "Sophia, I'm not trying to interfere. I'm just here for Lukas—"

"For Lukas?" Sophia's laughter—sharp and bitter—burst forth. "You may say you're not be after Max now, but what about later? You think he won't fall for someone like you? You need to think long and hard about your presence here before you push me too far."

Lukas stepped back, eyes darting between the two, bewildered by Sophia's ferocity. "Come on, this isn't necessary. Eliza is—"

"Delightful company, is it?" Sophia interrupted, her voice tinged with venom. "Just remember, Eliza, the estate isn't a place for your kind of fun. You aren't welcome there."

As she turned on her heel, Lukas reached for Sophia's arm, but she shrugged him off, storming down the hall.

Merlin watched, his feline heart heavy with the weight of the chaos unfolding. Secrets spilled like poisoned wine, and with each hiss of anger from Sophia, the stakes climbed higher in this twisted web of desire and betrayal.

With a final flick of his tail, Merlin approached his human, mewing softly to get her attention. Eliza knelt, her gaze falling upon him, and for a moment, the chaos melted away.

"What is it, little one?" she asked, brushing her fingers gently along his back.

"Come with me." Merlin's green eyes glimmered as he urged her to follow him, padding down the corridor, glancing back every so often to make sure she was behind him.

But in the thick of emotion, Sophia had retreated to the far end of the barn, her anger hanging in the air like fog. She leaned against an empty stall, staring out into the fading light of dusk, her thoughts spiraling. "He doesn't get it," she muttered to herself, the weight of her brother's bond with Eliza heavy on her soul. "I can't let her charm him."

Back with Eliza, Merlin halted, his gaze fixed on the doorway where the secretary had been moments before. "You need to know what I heard," he seemed to say, his whiskers twitching in anticipation.

Eliza caught up. "Merlin, what's wrong? You look like you've seen a ghost."

As if summoned by the tension of unspoken words, the secretary reappeared, flanked by a couple of stable hands.

The Spanish Riding School Incident

Her voice, although moderate, sliced through the air in whispers. "We need to prepare for the police. They'll be here blitzing in like storm clouds, and there's no stopping them now."

Merlin moved closer to Eliza, sensing a brewing storm in her eyes. She drew a steadying breath, grounding herself.

Merlin took her to the cloak that was draped on the stall door. "Look," he said, "check around the buttons."

Eliza's fingers trembled slightly as she reached for the cloak. When she inspected the buttons, something caught her eye—a wisp of long, golden hair tangled among the golden embroidery. She pulled it gently, revealing more strands that shimmered. She realized that this hair did not belong to her. It was a clear sign that another had been here, covering themselves in the very guise that had once held the promise of safety and protection.

"Merlin," she murmured, lifting the strands to eye level, her voice barely above a whisper. "This... this belongs to someone else." She turned to Merlin, "Do you recognize it? Is there someone you know who might have worn this?"

She offered the hair to Merlin's nose.

"Sophia," he said.

Merlin's expression deepened into a frown. "I cannot say for certain, but the presence of this hair changes matters," he replied, his voice growing low and grave. "We must tread carefully, Eliza. This cloak may hold more than mere threads of fabric."

Eliza swallowed hard, her eyes darting back to the cloak as if expecting it to whisper the secrets it bore. "You can't be serious, Merlin. We can't just dismiss this," she insisted, her voice betraying her rising apprehension. "What if she starts watching us?"

"Enough with the worry, Eliza!" Merlin snapped

suddenly, his eyes glinting with an intensity that demanded her full attention. "We need to focus. This isn't just a cloak—it's a clue. If we want to unravel the truth behind all of this, we must be strategic. You've allowed yourself to be caught up in fear when you should be sharpening your mind." He stepped closer, the tension between them palpable, urging her to remain steadfast even as he heard her heart thundering in her chest. "What matters now is figuring out what this means for us. Look beyond the fear, and let's get to the core of it."

"I know," Eliza replied, her mind whirling with the implications of what Merlin told her the secretary had shared before.

Outside, in the hallway, Sophia stood off from the crown watching Eliza and Merlin. She moved her mouth silently, grappling with an arsenal of unspoken words. Every moment Eliza spent with Max felt like another stab to her heart.

Suddenly, Lukas pushed through the haze of tension, hands raised defensively. "Sophia, calm down. Let's be civil."

"Civil?" she spat, anger feeding into her words. "You don't understand what she represents! It's not just about you or me; it's about blood! I refuse to sit quiet while she wields influence over our history."

Just as he opened his mouth to argue back, Merlin emerged from the shadows, pawing insistently, as though he had become the ambassador of the very secrets swirling within the barn.

Eliza turned, catching sight of him, confusion at the forefront. "What is it, Merlin?" she asked softly, instinctively kneeling.

With a flick of his tufted tail and a resolute gaze, Merlin

led her deeper into the heart of the barn, leaving behind the storm brewing in the hallway. Behind them, Lukas and Sophia still argued.

Just then, the heavy barn door creaked open, causing the air to shift with urgency. A couple of uniformed officers walked in, their expressions grim but resolute. They observed the disarray of the barn, taking note of the scattered tools and the shadows that loomed.

Merlin, sensing their approach, hurriedly took two steps back, but it was too late. The officers had already spotted the cloak lying forlornly at the entrance of the stall.

"Hey, over here!" one officer called, drawing his partner's attention. They both moved closer, kneeling to inspect the cloak.

"What do you see?" the second officer murmured, brushing debris aside.

Eliza turned to look for Sophia, But she was gone.

Chapter Eleven

Max glanced down the darkened corridor, his heart pounding louder than the soft thud of footsteps behind him. Eliza's shadow danced along the stone walls, and for a moment, he felt a rush of exhilaration—this was their secret.

"Shh," he whispered, glancing back toward the grand living room where his sister, Sophia, was watching TV. Laughter echoed from the screen, a discordant symphony, and Max felt a pang of longing to be part of that world again. But not tonight. Tonight was reserved for Eliza.

As she and Merlin slipped into his dimly lit room, he closed the door softly, the click echoing in the stillness. The moonlight filtered through the window, casting silvery patterns on the floor—a haven carved from the darkness that surrounded them.

Eliza moved toward the window, pushing aside the curtains slightly. "It feels wrong, sneaking in like this," she said, her voice laced with anxiety but tinted with excitement.

Max moved closer, resting a hand on her arm. "It's not

wrong, not when it's about us. My sister is just overprotective. You know what she's like."

Eliza looked at him, her eyes glimmering in the faint light. "Something's been bothering me, Max. It's about that farrier. You know what the others say about Hans. It wasn't just anyone who wanted him dead. What do you think happened?"

Max shrugged. "Hans was quite a lothario. He could have been killed by many people—a jealous husband, for one."

"Merlin doesn't like me being here either," she replied, casting a glance toward the corner where her cat lounged, eyeing her warily.

Max chuckled softly, shaking his head. "Merlin is just grumpy because someone else is stealing his attention."

"Right," she mused, crouching down to scratch behind the cat's ears. Merlin blinked slowly, the hint of a purr rumbling deep within him as he relented a little, though his eyes remained skeptical. "Careful," Merlin grumbled.

Max shifted, leaning against the desk cluttered with half-written notes and abandoned sketches. "What if we just talked? About Hans, about everything. I don't want you to feel like you have to sneak around."

Eliza straightened, dusting her hands off against her jeans. "Talking leads to more trouble, Max. You know how furious Sophia would be if she found out I was here."

"I don't care," he said, his voice simmering just above a whisper. "I need you to know that this—what we have—is worth it."

Max crossed the distance between them, touching the sides of her face to brush her hair behind her ear, letting his fingers linger for a moment longer than necessary.

"Lets leave all that behind tonight."

Chapter Twelve

Schwarzkopf sat in his cramped laboratory, the scent of acetone and sulfur mingling with the damp air, concentrating. The clutter of glass beakers and test tubes encircled him like a fortress, a sanctuary from the outside world. But now the sanctity of his space was shattered by the sound of his phone ringing—an incessant, jarring intrusion. He glanced at the screen and scowled; it was Officer Richards, the lead investigator on the Hans case.

"Schwarzkopf, we need to speak with you," Richards said, his voice cool but taut, like the string of a drawn bow. "Can you meet us at the precinct?"

"Yes, of course," he replied, though unease twisted in his gut. What did they want from him? He had done nothing wrong—yet.

The drive to the precinct felt longer than it really was, each traffic light an eternity, each moment ticking by like a metronome of dread. Schwarzkopf parked his car and stepped into the station, the sterile atmosphere, punctuated by the buzz of fluorescent lights, only added to his anxiety.

He was escorted to an interrogation room—cold, stark, and isolating. The walls felt like they closed in as he sat down across from Richards and another officer, a young woman with sharp, piercing eyes.

"Thank you for coming," the officer said, folding her hands as she leaned forward slightly. "We want to talk about Hans Meyer."

Schwarzkopf swallowed hard. "I heard about his incident. It was tragic."

"Tragic indeed," Richards replied, studying him closely. "Hans was a whistleblower, was he not? Concerned about the condition of the horses whose feed you were analyzing."

"Yes, he had his concerns," Schwarzkopf found himself saying, each word feeling like sandpaper against his throat. "But I assure you, I had no intention of harming him."

"Then why," started the young officer, retrieving a phone from an evidence bag and placing it on the table, "did he send this message just days before his death?"

Schwarzkopf's eyebrows jerked up as he read the screen: "I know what you did, and I'm not afraid to go to the authorities. The horses deserve better. If anything happens to me, they'll know you had a motive."

A heavy silence descended as the chemist absorbed the words. He glanced nervously at Richards and the female officer, searching their faces for any sign of accusation. "I didn't—he was just...he was just trying to intimidate me," he stammered. "We were in disagreement over the issue of the food. It could have been caused by climate change. I still need time to conduct tests, and I can understand why, but—"

"Upset enough to think you might have killed him?" Richards questioned, raising an eyebrow. "You received a substantial payment recently, didn't you? One that might look like a payoff to someone in Hans's position."

"No, I—" Schwarzkopf started, but the words stumbled in his throat. He needed to justify the payment, which had been legitimate, after all. A grant for research that had, ironically, begun to reveal the flaws in the horse feed recipe. "I did receive a grant for my research! I was working on a solution! That kind of money isn't uncommon in this field—"

"Except Hans was aware of it," the young officer interjected. "He knew about your findings regarding the imbalance. You stand to lose a lot in reputation and funding if this gets out, don't you?"

"Do you think I'd risk my career over a few horses?" he shot back, desperation creeping in as frustration fueled his defense. "I had nothing to gain from harming Hans." You may want to question the feed vendor. They have the most at stake."

"But you did have something to lose," Richards pointed out steadily. "And that's why we're here."

Schwarzkopf felt the pressure tighten around him, like a noose. "You think I'm the only one who cared about the horses? I'm not a monster! Hans...he was passionate, but his approach was reckless. I didn't even agree with him on many points— Hooves are not the only indicator of bad feed."

Richards leaned back in his chair, studying the chemist's face for any tells, the tiniest crack in his facade. "You mention passionate. People can act irrationally when feeling cornered. Didn't Hans confront you in public months ago, after you received that funding? Did that light the fire?"

The memories cascaded unbidden—the argument at a barn, Hans's face flushed with indignation, then his voice raised for all to hear as Hans railed against Schwarzkopf's findings and the dangers posed to the horses. It had been a moment of embarrassment. "That was just... that was just a disagreement," the researcher maintained weakly, sinking further into his chair.

"Disagreements can lead to extreme outcomes, Schwarzkopf," the female officer pressed, leaning in. "Especially when one party stands to benefit monetarily."

Officer Richards twirled a pencil in his hand reflectively. "Thank you for your time, Dr. Schwarzkopf. We will get back to you if you need anything further."

Chapter Thirteen

Max insisted that Eliza brazenly accompany him downstairs after they'd spent the night together. Imagine Eliza's surprise when Sophia arrived and then placed a delicate porcelain tray on the table in the mansion's breakfast room. The tray's edges were adorned with intricate floral designs. The afternoon sunlight streamed through the window, catching the sparkles of sugar dust cascading over the tea cakes, each a masterpiece of tempting delight. They were small, yet exquisite, each topped with a glossy berry glaze that shimmered like dew on a summer morning.

"Good morning, Eliza!" Sophia chirped, her voice bright and cheerful as she arranged the pastries with exaggerated care. "I hope you're in the mood for a treat. I made your favorite—lemon cream tarts and lavender-infused scones! Aren't they simply beautiful? I know how much you like Frau Schmidt's bakery. I hope my baking is on the same level."

Eliza managed a smile, her heart fluttering nervously as she watched Sophia fuss over the food. "They look amazing,

Sophia. I wish I had the appetite to enjoy them. What a lovely surprise!"

Lukas leaned back in his chair, arms crossed, his expression one of mild interest. "You really went all out, didn't you? Even the coffee looks like something from a café in Paris." He surveyed the rich, dark brew steaming in fine china cups adorned with gold filigree.

"Oh, thank you! I pulled out mamma's special china and used the unique blend you recommended last time," Sophia said, pouring the coffee with a theatrical flourish. "Just a touch of cream, if you please?" She held the pitcher towards Eliza, whose hands trembled, showing how nervous she was as she reached for it.

Merlin hopped up onto the table, his fur a mottled blend of orange stripes, and eyed the cream with tangible excitement. "Merlin! Not on the table!" Eliza exclaimed, though her tone was more amused than upset. Sophia's laugh was light and airy, masking the deeper intentions that twisted in her mind.

"What an impudent little rascal you are," Sophia teased, her fingers brushing against Merlin's soft fur as she poured a small puddle of cream into a saucer beside him. The cat dove in, lapping eagerly, completely oblivious to the tension simmering in the air.

"I'm so worth it," Merlin intoned and then wiped his mouth with his paw.

Lukas leaned forward. "Sophia, you really must have made these just for Eliza! They won't be nearly as good without her approval." He shot a teasing grin at Eliza, who felt an involuntary flush creep up her cheeks.

"Oh, I wouldn't dare take credit for this spread if Eliza doesn't want it—although I do think she'll find it hard to resist," Sophia replied, her eyes glistening with hidden glee. She forced a smile wide enough to conceal any discontent.

Eliza bit her lip, her stomach churning nervously. "I mean, I didn't have breakfast at all. I might just sample a few." She reached for the closest scone, its surface glistening with a light glaze and sprinkled with bits of dried lavender. The aroma wafted up to her, intoxicating and sweet.

"Of course! Life is too short not to indulge," Sophia encouraged, her voice syrupy. "And I assure you, they're fresh from the oven. You won't find anything quite like this at the academy or even Frau Schmidt's, I promise."

Eliza's mind wandered back to that glorious night in the mansion, spent in the arms of her rich young admirer, Max. The passion had been intense, his hands exploring every curve of her body as she tangled her fingers in his hair. She could still feel the sensual tingle of his lips trailing kisses down her neck, his teeth grazing her sensitive skin.

As they moved together in a frenzied dance of lust, Eliza knew she was the most desired woman in the world. Afterwards, they collapsed onto the plush silk sheets, chests heaving and hearts pounding. Eliza glanced at the vain portrait of his spinster sister on the wall, her sour expression almost comical in contrast to the heated glances Eliza exchanged with her lover. In that moment, Eliza felt powerful, beautiful, and utterly irresistible. It was a night she would never forget.

Now here in the breakfast room, Max took a sip of his coffee, eyes observing Sophia like a hawk. "So, what's the occasion for this elaborate spread? You're usually so busy with your other endeavors."

"Oh, you know how it is," Sophia replied, a sparkle in her eyes that was not entirely genuine. "Just wanted to treat Eliza after her few days of hard riding. We've all been feeling rather cooped up lately, haven't we? And then that horrid incident with Hans yesterday."

Eliza dared a glance at Max, finding him contemplating Sophia with an unreadable expression. "The pastries are really kind of you," she managed. "I appreciate the thought, Sophia."

Max reached for Eliza's hand under the table and squeezed it, only to feel Merlin swat it away.

"Anytime!" Sophia beamed, a touch too brightly. "And you know, Eliza, you really should enjoy these. Life can be so much sweeter when we take a moment to be indulgent."

Merlin, having sated his cream craving, now curled into a tight ball near the table, watching them with half-lidded eyes as if this mundane tableau was mere entertainment.

Sensing a shift in atmosphere, Max attempted to steer the conversation away from anything too heavy. "What about the area showing artwork next month? Are you all prepared for your entries, Sophia?"

Sophia nodded vigorously, a faux excitement radiating from her. "Absolutely. I, for one, can't wait to showcase my talents. I've been practicing, you'll see!" She winked at Eliza, who felt apprehensive yet intrigued.

Eliza quickly swallowed a bite of scone, the flavor bursting on her tongue—but it was a bittersweet taste, an uneasy lingering that made her mind race.

Max sat up a bit straighter. "And what about your new plans? The ones with the academy? You know—every time I hear you talk about them, I can't help but be curious."

"Oh, my brother, you know I like to keep some things under wraps!" Sophia laughed, her voice a layer too thin. "But you'll find out soon enough. It'll be a revelation!"

Another sip from Max's coffee cup punctuated the moment, as silence consumed them momentarily. Eliza looked down, inspecting her plate suddenly overwhelmed with choices, a bountiful spread that began to feel like too much for her.

"I suppose we must all make sacrifices for our dreams, right?" Max finally mused, glancing at Eliza.

"Exactly!" Sophia chimed, launching right into a story about sacrifices she had made, charm radiating from her words, yet there was a slight tightening at the corners of her mouth. "I've had to bypass so many social events lately, but I tell myself each moment spent working towards my goals is worth it!"

Eliza, unable to shake the unease gnawing at her, replied softly, "Sometimes it's good to find balance, too. After all, friends matter just as much as achievements."

"I think it's admirable," Max interjected, humor lighting his gaze. "Especially when it comes to scones! Perhaps I could join you both in this pursuit—what do you say, Eliza? More coffee, more tea cakes, more study dates?"

Sophia giggled, "Now that sounds like a perfect idea! Picture us, bonding over delectable pastries, ignoring the huge world outside. A cozy bubble!"

Eliza nodded, though her heart pulsed erratically at how the veil of camaraderie hung so lightly. Perhaps it was just her guilt, but there was something about Sophia's laughter that rang slightly out of tune.

"Merlin, would you like to join us for tea, too?" Max teased, bringing the conversation back around to the cat. "Perhaps you could use a break from all your travels."

Merlin sniffed at the pastries and curled his lip, then responded with a yawn, exposing a his upper palette. This made Eliza chuckle despite herself.

But somewhere in the back of her mind, a quiet whisper beckoned, urging her to tread carefully.

The Spanish Riding School Incident

An hour later, Eliza squirmed in the saddle, desperately trying to focus on Lukas's instructions while battling the urgent rumblings in her stomach. Lukas had shown up right on time as always. She wished he'd been late because she felt like she needed more time in the bathroom. "I, um, think I need a quick break," she stammered, backing away slightly.

"Break? Already?" Lukas raised an eyebrow, concern creeping into his voice. "Is it the heat, or are you just nervous?"

"It's a bit of both," she forced a laugh. "I've got, um, a summer bug or something."

Merlin, lounging atop a hay bale, snickered loudly. "Summer bug? More like summer hussy! I bet the only thing you're catching today is an embarrassing exit!"

Eliza glared at the cat. "You're supposed to be on my side, Merlin!"

"Oh please, what's a little fun if not at your expense?" Merlin purred mockingly.

Lukas frowned, eyeing Eliza with concern. "Seriously, are you okay? We can take a break, no problem."

"No, no!" Eliza insisted, feeling the heat rise in her cheeks. "I'm fine. Let's just keep going."

She squeezed her legs tighter around the horse, willing her body to cooperate. But just as Lukas resumed their lesson, another wave hit her. She winced, muttering, "Oh no, not again…"

"Uh oh, someone's in trouble!" Merlin yowled, rolling over dramatically. "You realize you look like a cartoon character right now?"

"Shut it, Merlin," Eliza hissed, trying to keep her composure. "Lukas, I really think we should—"

But before she could finish, her stomach betrayed her.

"I'll be right back!" she blurted out, her voice a mix of urgency and embarrassment as she leapt off the horse.

"Hey, wait!" Lukas called after her, but she was already sprinting toward the barn bathroom.

"Great lesson plan, huh!" Merlin called after, nearly falling off the hay bale in laughter. "Maybe next time opt for some digestion-friendly treats!"

As Eliza emerged from the barn, looking pale, Lukas was waiting by the fence hold Bixo, looking worried.

"I'm so sorry, Lukas! This is mortifying," Eliza interrupted, scrunching her face in embarrassment.

He chuckled softly, attempting to ease the tension. "Look, if it helps, I've had worse experiences during a lesson. Once, I decided to eat too many beans before riding."

Eliza blinked. "Did you...?"

"Let's just say the horses were not the only ones running that day," he confessed, a smile creeping onto his face.

"Okay, well, at least I'm not the only one who's had a messy moment," she said with a faint grin.

Merlin chimed in from his perch, "Beans or tea cakes, it seems like all the good riders have their secrets!"

Chapter Fourteen

Eliza made her way to the university, where Professor Berlin's office awaited. She took a deep breath, excited to hear about the latest mushroom dye findings from the esteemed scholar. Merlin had decided to sleep in that morning.

Knocking on the door, Eliza heard the familiar voice of Professor Berlin call out, "Come in, come in!" She opened the door and stepped inside, greeted by the comforting smell of old books and the professor's pipe tobacco.

"Ah, Eliza! I was hoping you'd stop by. Please, have a seat," Berlin said, gesturing to the chair in front of his desk. "I'm eager to show you more of what I've learned from the batch we last cultivated.

Eliza settled into the chair, her eyes shining with enthusiasm. "Professor, what a breakthrough. The technique you've been experimenting with has yielded remarkable results. The color is more vibrant and the dye itself is much more stable than our previous attempts."

Berlin leaned forward, "It's all so fascinating, my dear."

Eliza listened to his detailed explanation of his findings.

His hands gesturing animatedly as he described the intricate process he had developed. She jotted down a note from time to time.

Eliza couldn't help but notice the professor's eyes occasionally drifting downward, lingering on her chest. She felt a faint flush creep up her neck, but she was determined to maintain her composure and professional demeanor.

Berlin sat back in his chair, a satisfied smile spreading across his face. "Eliza, my dear, this is remarkable work. We should be very proud of our accomplishments."

Eliza beamed, her heart swelling with pride. "Thank you, Professor. I'm grateful for the opportunity to work on this project and contribute to our understanding of textile dyes."

Berlin nodded, his gaze still fixed on Eliza. "Yes, yes, of course. Your contributions have been invaluable, my dear. Tell me, have you given any thought to the future? Where do you see this research leading?"

Eliza paused, considering the question. "Well, I believe there are countless applications for this dye, both in the textile industry and beyond. Imagine the possibilities if we could replicate these results on a larger scale. The potential for new and vibrant clothing, upholstery, and even artistic expression is truly exciting. The organic producers will be impressed. Something old is new again."

Berlin's eyes twinkled with interest. "Ah, yes, the possibilities are indeed intriguing. And you, my dear Eliza, are the key to unlocking this potential."

Eliza felt a flutter in her stomach, unsure of how to interpret the professor's words. Before she responded, Berlin leaned forward, his gaze now fixed on her intently.

"Tell me, Eliza, have you ever considered the personal

The Spanish Riding School Incident

applications of your work? The ways in which it could enrich your own life, perhaps even in unexpected ways?"

Eliza's brow arched, confusion evident in her expression. "I'm afraid I don't quite understand, Professor. What do you mean?"

Berlin chuckled, a mischievous glint in his eye. "My dear, I believe there are opportunities here that go beyond the academic realm. Opportunities that could bring you personal fulfillment, not just professional success."

Eliza felt a pang of unease, unsure of where this conversation was heading. She shifted in her seat, her hands clasping the edge of the chair.

"I'm not sure I follow, Professor. My focus has been on the research and its potential impact. I haven't really considered any personal implications."

Berlin leaned back in his chair, his gaze vacillating from Eliza's face and then her chest. "Well, perhaps it's time you did. After all, you are a young, vibrant woman, with so much to offer the world. And I, as your mentor, am here to guide you, to help you see the full scope of what you can achieve."

Eliza swallowed hard. The professor's words, and the way he was looking at her, made her deeply uncomfortable. She rose from her seat, her breath had suddenly become much more shallow.

"Thank you, Professor, for your kind words and for your support of my research. I appreciate your guidance, but I think it's best if I take my leave for now. I have much to consider, and I don't want to take up any more of your time."

Berlin's expression shifted, a flash of disappointment crossing his features, but he quickly covered it with a smile. "Of course, my dear. Please, take all the time you need. I'm here if you ever want to discuss this further."

Eliza nodded. She hurried out of the office, the weight of the professor's words weighing heavily on her. As she walked home, her thoughts were consumed by the unsettling encounter, and she couldn't shake the feeling that something had shifted, that her relationship with the esteemed scholar was no longer as straightforward as she had once believed.

When Eliza returned to her cozy apartment, she thought she would be greeted by the familiar sight of Merlin, her beloved cat, curled up on his favorite spot on the windowsill. But as she approached, she noticed something peculiar—a small, cat-sized purple cloak draped over his carrier.

Eliza gently picked up the cloak, running her fingers over the soft, velvety fabric. "Merlin, what on earth have you been up to?"

There was no answer.

Suddenly, Eliza's eyes went wide, and she began to frantically search the apartment, calling out Merlin's name. "Merlin? Merlin, where are you?"

She checked every nook and cranny, but the cat was nowhere to be found. The purple cloak lay abandoned on the floor.

Had Merlin wandered off on some feline adventure, only to return with this peculiar garment? Or had something more sinister occurred, leaving her beloved companion lost or in danger?

Panic gripped her as she paced the apartment, her thoughts racing. She had to find Merlin, no matter what. The thought of him out there, alone and possibly in harm's way, was too much to bear.

Grabbing her coat and hat, Eliza rushed out the door,

determined to retrace her steps and search every corner of the neighborhood for any sign of her furry companion.

Eliza texted Max from an Uber. *Meet me at your gate. It's an emergency.*

She explained what had happened to Merlin when she fell into Max's arms holding him tight and she pounded his shoulders.

Max winced at each pounding fist, feeling the urgency in Eliza's frantic demands. He knew better than to argue with her in this state; her passion for Merlin is one of the many reasons he respected her. With a swift nod, he pulled her towards the garage and pushed her into his Ferrari. The Ferrari's engine roared to life with a throaty growl that echoed Eliza's own fierce determination.

"Let's go get Merlin back," Max said, his voice steady and resolute. The tires screeched as they peeled away from the property, leaving a trail of rubber on the asphalt. The car navigated the winding streets with precision, as if it too understood the gravity of the situation.

As they speed away from the Muller estate, Eliza's anger simmered into a focused calm. She gritted her teeth, promising herself that whoever was behind this would regret their actions.

They had no luck finding Merlin in town. But it was then that Eliza remembered her cat had a tracking chip in his collar. She logged onto the app on her phone.

"I've never had to deal with this before," she sobbed.

The locator showed that Merlin was actually back at the Muller estate! Max made a U-turn in the middle of a busy intersection. The Ferrari ate up the distance, and soon the grandiose place loomed large before them, its imposing gates standing as a silent challenge. Max didn't hesitate, driving straight through the gate after clicking on his gate fob several hundred yards out. They zoomed in.

"Let's ask Sophia," he suggested, his tone leaving no room for question.

Eliza and Max parked the car and made their way to Sophia's wing, following the signal from Merlin's chip. They reached Sophia's door, and without a moment's hesitation, Eliza burst in, ready to confront whatever lay ahead to bring Merlin home. The room was opulent, filled with artifacts and rich tapestries that spoke of Sophia's wealth and eccentric tastes. Eliza's eyes, however, are not drawn to the grandeur but to the small, familiar form curled up on a velvet cushion near the fireplace.

"Merlin!" Eliza exclaims, her voice a mix of relief and fury. The cat lifted his head slowly, his eyes unfocused. It was obvious he'd been sedated.

Sophia Muller, a woman of refined beauty and notorious for her love of collecting rare items, rose from her chaise lounge with a measured grace. "Ah, Eliza, I see you've found your precious Merlin," she says, her voice dripping with condescension. "I must say, he's been the perfect guest."

Max positioned himself protectively beside Eliza, his gaze fixed on Sophia. "What's the meaning of this, Sophia? You had no right to take Merlin without permission," he challenges, his voice laced with a hard edge.

Eliza strode across the room, scooping Merlin into her arms, and checked all of his limbs and belly to make sure he was ok. The cat drunkenly licked her face eagerly, purring with joy. "Curiosity doesn't give you the right to take what isn't yours," Eliza retorts, her eyes flashing with indignation.

Sophia sighed, a theatrical display of regret. "I suppose you're right. Consider it a lapse in judgment. Next time you may not find him as easily. Especially if you continue to see my brother. But now that you're here, won't you stay for some tea? We could discuss terms for Merlin's extended visit."

"Why? So you try to poison me again?"

Max stepped forward, his jaw set. "There will be no terms, Sophia. Eliza and Merlin are leaving, and this better not happen again."

Sophia's eyes narrow, a hint of her well-known tenacity shining through. "Max, always the knight in shining armor. Very well, they may leave. But Eliza, you and I are not finished. There's a game afoot, and I expect you to play your part."

Eliza, holding Merlin close, turned to leave, not giving Sophia the satisfaction of a response. As they exited the room, Sophia called out, "Until we meet again, dear Eliza!"

As they made their way out of the house, through the kitchen, Eliza noticed several bottles of a pink medicine lined up on a ledge. It was Ex-Lax. She shook her head, too preoccupied by her cat's rescue to pay it much mind.

The gates of the Muller estate closed behind them with a resounding clang. As they drove away, Eliza looks down at Merlin, who seemed none the worse for wear, and smiled. "Let's go home, boy," she says, her voice softening for the first time since Merlin went missing.

As the Ferrari roared down the road carrying them away from the property, Eliza felt a sense of closure. Yet, she couldn't shake the feeling that this encounter with Sophia was merely the beginning of a larger, more intricate game. But for tonight, Merlin was safe, and that's all that mattered.

Chapter Fifteen

Feeling the need for a sugar rush, Eliza told Max to take them straightaway to Frau Schmidt's bakery which was across the street from her apartment.

Now the aroma of fresh bread and cinnamon hung thick in the air, a comforting cloud against Merlin's fur. His purr rumbled deep within him, a contented counterpoint to the rhythmic thump of Eliza's footsteps as they navigated the sidewalk of the bustling streets of Vienna.

He, Merlin, the most magnificent of felines, was nestled securely in the crook of her arm, his emerald eyes half-closed in blissful contentment. He was home.

He'd been lost, stolen away from his beloved Eliza, trapped in a gilded cage within the ostentatious walls of the Muller mansion.

. . .

The indignity of it all! But fate, as it often did, had intervened.

Merlin had stumbled upon a secret within those opulent walls, a truth that could very well unravel the mysteries that had plagued their lives recently.

Although he liked the refuge in Sophia Muller's room, he knew that she had ulterior motives. He had been drawn by the plush carpet and the alluring scent of lavender. Sophia, much to Merlin's disgust, had been engaged in a vigorous workout, her grunts and groans echoing off the marble walls. It was during one particularly strenuous set, as she lay panting on her yoga mat, that she'd uttered the words that sent chills down the cat's spine.

"I can't believe I did it," she'd gasped, her voice hoarse with exertion. "But it had to be done. They can't find out."

Find out what? The question had clawed at Merlin's curiosity. He'd shifted closer, his sedated ears pricked, next catching snippets of a hurried conversation on her phone.

"...hidden...the stables...never find it..."

The stables! Could she be talking about...? But before he regained his full consciousness to puzzle out the meaning, the sound of a Eliza and Max bursting into the room was the next thing he remembered.

Now, safe in Eliza's embrace, the memory of that overheard conversation reminded him of how erratic Sophia was. He had to tell Eliza, had to find a way to communicate the danger lurking beneath the surface of the Mullers' seemingly idyllic world.

Eliza, oblivious to the turmoil brewing within her feline companion, stopped before the inviting warmth of Frau Schmidt's bakery. The scent of freshly baked bread, warm sugar, and yeast hit them in a glorious wave.

"Now, what will we have today?" Eliza murmured, her voice laced with the same affectionate tone one might use with a child.

Merlin, master of manipulation that he was, rubbed his head against her cheek, letting out a soft meow. He knew his purrs were her weakness. "I'll have the sardines with a side of cream."

"Oh, you deserve a feast after your ordeal, my darling," she cooed, her eyes sparkling with unshed tears of relief.

Minutes later, they emerged, their arms laden with a brown paper bag overflowing with goodies—flaky apple strudels, delicate cream horns, and a small, pungent tin of sardines, especially for Merlin.

As they made their way back to Max's car, Max said he would see them up to her apartment.

. . .

"I'm just so glad to have been able to help you," Max said.

"We're alright, Max, thanks to you," Eliza assured him, her voice laced with gratitude. "A little shaken, but we're together again."

Max nodded, his gaze still lingering on Merlin. "Good, good. Listen, there's something you two need to see. Come with me."

He ushered them towards Eliza's apartment building, a sense of urgency underlying his movements. As soon as they were safely inside Eliza's apartment, Max pulled out his phone, his face grim.

"Lukas just messaged. They found something at the stables—in Snowflake's stall, to be precise." He held up a picture on his phone. A small, silver charm, shaped like a miniature dagger, glinted on the screen.

Max frowned. "Unfortunately, I know that charm."

Merlin's ears twitched. He recognized it too.

Max grabbed Eliza's hand. "We need to go to the station now. Get Merlin's carrier."

"But I haven't had a chance to eat," Merlin protested.

. . .

Once at the station Merlin watched the scene unfold with a mixture of curiosity and trepidation. He knew, with a certainty that only a cat could possess, that the charm and Sophia's cryptic words were all pieces of a larger puzzle.

As he looked from the stern faces of the officers to Eliza's pale countenance, he knew he was the only one who could put those pieces together. The question was, how could he possibly tell them what he knew? His mind had not cleared yet.

Merlin observed the officers carefully, his feline instincts sharpening as the tension in the room escalated. A stout officer, whose badge glinted under the overhead lights, maintained a stern expression.

Max raised a hand, calming Eliza with a glance, and leaned closer to the officers. "Listen, while Eliza gathers her thoughts, why don't you show us what you've found?"

The taller officer exhaled wearily, as if considering the level of detail he could afford to share. "This charm, do you know where it came from?"

"It belongs to my sister. It's a trinket that was passed down from our grandmother."

. . .

"We found it in the stall where the murder took place."

Eliza turned to Max, "Was your sister mad at Hans?"

Max looked down at the ground.

"Well, it was because of Hans that she lost her leg."

"How?" Merlin questioned.

Max grew quiet before he answered. "Years ago Hans allowed her too close to a fractious mare while he shod the horse. The mare kicked her high in the leg. The break never healed correctly. After months of treatment, it got infected and had to be amputated. She was devastated and never forgave him."

Merlin shook his head, trying to shake off the drugs. "I just remembered something. Didn't Sophia want Hans to take her to the upcoming extravaganza? I heard her muttering about that while she had me in her room."

Max held up his hand. "Don't be ridiculous. She can't dance with that leg of hers. No way would she have been after him to act as an escort to such a fine event."

"But what about this charm?" the police officer pressed.

"Oh that? Sophia goes over to the Academy all the time to visit the horses. She probably lost it while she was petting Snowflake," Max offered.

Merlin growled softly. Eliza knew her cat didn't accept this explanation.

Chapter Sixteen

The grand hall of the Spanish Riding School hummed with anticipation. Crystal chandeliers cast dazzling diamonds of light onto the pristine white sand below, where Max Muller, astride one of the magnificent Lipizzaner stallions, seemed to glide rather than ride. Eliza rode Snowflake right next to him. Lukas stood in the middle giving them commands while narrating to the audience.

The air vibrated with the poignant melody of Mozart's Violin Concerto No. 5, a counterpoint to the rhythmic thud of hooves.

She watched as Max, every inch the consummate equestrian, guided his steed through intricate steps and airs above the ground while she performed more basic maneuvers on the ground.

He was elegance personified, his black riding jacket molded to his form as effortlessly as his white breeches clung to his powerful thighs. Eliza had never seen him so at ease, so completely in his element. The tension that usually tightened his jaw was gone, replaced by a look of pure joy.

Tonight was a testament to the Muller family legacy, a celebration of their beloved Lipizzaners. The aging stallion, Snowflake, once a renowned performer in his own right, was being brought out of retirement for one last dance. And Eliza, the rank amateur, was deemed worthy enough to be his partner.

As the final notes of the concerto faded away, the audience erupted into thunderous applause. Max, bowing low in the saddle, guided his stallion towards the gate, a satisfied smile on his lips. Eliza kept riding alongside him as they exited the arena.

"Max, that was breathtaking!" she exclaimed, her eyes sparkling. "You were incredible!"

"Thank you, Eliza," he replied, his smile becoming more broad as he dismounted. "Now the public has seen now good the training can be at this place. You have only had a handful of lessons with Lukas." He led his horse through the heavy velvet curtain that separated the arena from the stables, Eliza trailing behind. "But the real performance is yet to come. There is more to do with Snowflake."

The backstage area bustled with grooms and handlers, the air thick with the scents of hay, leather, and nervous horses. Snowflake, a magnificent creature with a coat as white as his namesake, walked with Eliza and then suddenly stopped. He held his head high, nostrils flaring. Eliza felt a tremor of unease around the powerful animal.

Suddenly, a strident voice cut through the organized chaos.

"Max! Darling, you were magnificent!"

Sophia, a whirlwind of blood red silk and expensive perfume, swept into the stable.

"Sophia," Max greeted, his tone even. "I trust you are enjoying the evening?"

The Spanish Riding School Incident

"Divine, darling, simply divine," Sophia gushed, her gaze sweeping over the stable until it landed on Eliza. Her smile tightened. "Ah, Miss Bennett. Preparing for the second round of your grand debut, I see."

"Indeed," Eliza replied coolly, aware of the undercurrent of tension.

Sophia, however, seemed oblivious to the chill in the air. With a dramatic flourish, she produced a small velvet pouch from her purse. "Max, darling, be a dear and fetch me a glass of champagne from the hospitality bar would you?" she instructed, her eyes fixed on Eliza.

As Max retreated, Sophia approached Snowflake's stall, her movements deceptively casual. "He's a magnificent creature, isn't he?" she purred, reaching out to stroke the stallion's nose.

Snowflake, however, snorted and tossed his head, taking a startled step back. The movement, though subtle, did not escape Eliza's notice, nor Merlin's.

"He's not usually skittish," Eliza commented.

"Perhaps he senses my admiration," Sophia laughed, but the sound held a brittle edge. She untied the velvet pouch, revealing a collection of silver knives, each engraved with a different crest. "These belonged to our grandmother. I thought it might be auspicious to allow Snowflake to choose one for luck before his performance."

Before anyone could react, she'd scooped up a handful of the knives and extended one towards the stallion's throat. Snowflake reared back, whinnying in alarm.

"Sophia! What are you doing?!" Eliza exclaimed, her voice sharp with alarm.

Startled, Sophia dropped it. They clattered to the straw-covered floor, the sound amplified in the sudden silence. Snowflake trembled, his eyes wide with fear.

Eliza, her own pulse quickening, crouched down, her gaze sweeping the floor where the knives lay scattered. One, she noticed, was dented, as if it had been crushed under a heavy weight. This wasn't right. Something was very wrong.

"Sophia," she said quietly, her voice steady despite the tremor of apprehension that ran through her. "Why is Snowflake so frightened of you?"

Max had returned with glasses of champagne.

Sophia's eyes darted nervously between Eliza and her brother. Her carefully constructed façade began to crumble, revealing the fear and frustration beneath. "I don't understand," she stammered, her voice uncharacteristically small.

It was Max who broke the tense silence. "Sophia," he said, his voice dangerously soft, "I suggest you tell us what's going on. Now."

Tears welled in Sophia's eyes, but she met her brother's gaze with a defiant spark. "Fine!" she burst out, her voice cracking. "I'll tell you! It was Hans! That oafish, ungrateful..."

She cut herself off, her face flushing with anger. "He refused to escort me to tonight's event!" she finally spat, her voice thick with tears of humiliation.

"But Hans is dead!" Max's eyebrows shot up, clearly taken aback.

"I asked him, nicely, of course," Sophia continued, twisting her hands together. "Offered to pay him handsomely, even! But he refused!"

"And you're upset because...?" Eliza prompted gently, already suspecting the answer.

"Because it's my family's event!" Sophia cried, throwing her hands up in the air. "I thought surely even a lowly farrier like him would jump at the chance to escort a Muller!"

The Spanish Riding School Incident

A heavy silence descended upon them. Max stared at his sister, his expression unreadable. Eliza, however, felt a surge of fear for Sophia, despite her appalling behavior.

It was then that a soft meow broke the tension. Merlin materialized from the shadows, his eyes fixed on the scattered knives. He padded over to the dented one, sniffing it delicately before letting out a low growl.

Eliza exchanged a look with Max, a silent understanding passing between them. Merlin's behavior confirmed their suspicions. Sophia, in a fit of pique, had taken her anger out on Snowflake.

"Sophia," Max said finally, his voice low and dangerous. "You had no right to do that. Snowflake is a valuable animal, and more importantly, a part of our heritage here."

"But he's just a horse!" Sophia protested, her voice trembling and rising an octave. "And Hans... he insulted me! He treated me like..."

"Like you're not entitled to everything you want?" Eliza finished quietly.

Sophia's mouth snapped shut, her face flushing crimson.

"This isn't about Hans, Sophia," Max said, his voice firm. "This is about you. You need to take responsibility for your actions."

He knelt down and began to gather the knives, his movements precise and controlled. "Go home, Sophia," he said, his voice devoid of emotion. "We'll discuss this later."

Sophia, her face pale, stood frozen for a moment, then turned and fled, her expensive shoes slapping against the stable floor.

The silence that followed her departure was heavy, broken only by the soft whicker of horses in their stalls. Eliza crouched beside Snowflake, offering him a comforting pat. The stallion, sensing her empathy, lowered his head and nuzzled her hand.

"Don't worry, Snowflake," she murmured, stroking his velvety nose. "We need to finish our performance."

Max, who had been watching them, came to stand beside her, his gaze thoughtful. "Thank you, Eliza," he said softly. "For your understanding. I think our next step is to go to the police. My sister is not in her right mind and hasn't been for a long time."

Eliza met his gaze, her heart aching with a mixture of sympathy and something deeper, something she couldn't quite name. "It's alright, Max," she replied, her voice barely a whisper.

As she gazed at Max she knew one thing for certain. This night, already filled with unexpected twists and turns, was far from over.

Chapter Seventeen

Eliza picked up Merlin after dressing him in standard uniform of the Spanish Riding School and hoisted him onto the saddle in front of her on Snowflake. Max had his horse ready to go.

They entered the ring for their final performance of the evening and the audience was clapping in time with the music she gave a rueful smile to Max because they both knew what they had to do once the evening was over.

The ride would be bittersweet. Snowflake had settled down now that Sophia had left the premises. Eliza took a deep breath as the music swelled, the notes weaving an elegant tapestry that united her and Snowflake.

She urged the gelding into a graceful trot, her heart pounding with both anticipation and nostalgia. Max mirrored her movements, his horse gliding effortlessly beside them.

They began with a series of intricate figure eights, their horses weaving in perfect harmony—fluid, synchronized, like a dance choreographed by the stars themselves.

"Nice turn, Eliza!" Merlin called out, perched confidently on Snowflake's saddle. His whiskers twitched as he added, "Maybe stick to the riding and leave the pirouettes to the professionals!"

Ignoring the playful jab, Eliza grinned and coaxed Snowflake into a canter, the rhythm of their bodies flowing together.

They moved into an impressive stretch across the arena, both horses extending their strides in elegant arcs and matched each other stride for stride.

Max flashed her a triumphant smile as they transitioned into a trot that flowed seamlessly into a series of lateral work—the shoulder-ins and haunches-ins.

"Wow, I didn't know horses could dance like this! What's next, a tango?" Merlin quipped, his tail flicking with bemusement.

"Just focus, you furry distraction. We need to impress," Eliza replied, her voice steady as she executed a thrilling passage through the center of the arena, the audience's applause rising to a crescendo. She felt the energy coursing through her, every clap urging her on.

As they rounded a corner, Max, who had moved to the arena's center, performed a series of stunning jumps, each leap punctuated by the fervent cheers from the crowd.

Merlin, seemingly unfazed, added, "You know, if we fall, it's definitely your fault for dragging me into this chaotic circus!"

Eliza chuckled at Merlin's comments.

With a flourish, they came to a stunning stop, their horses piaffing slightly, nostrils flaring, as the audience erupted into applause.

Merlin leapt off the saddle, deeper into Eliza's arms, shaking his head, "Next time, let's find a safer hobby—like snoozing in sunbeams!"

The End

Thank you for reading this third book in our Stitches in Secrets cozy mystery series. The fourth book occurs in beautiful Scotland. If so motivated, please leave a review for us on KDP. It would be much appreciated.

Made in United States
North Haven, CT
14 November 2024